Stacey's Choice

Stacey's Choice
Ann M. Martin

AN
APPLE
PAPERBACK

SCHOLASTIC INC.
New York Toronto London Auckland Sydney

Cover art by Hodges Soileau

ISBN 0-590-45659-8

12 11 10 9 8 7 6 5 4 3 2 1   2 3 4 5 6 7/9

Printed in the U.S.A.   40

First Scholastic printing, October 1992

For Alexis, Fritzie, and Mimi

Stacey's Choice

CHAPTER 1

The dry leaves crunched under our sneakers.

"I just love autumn, don't you?" said Mallory Pike.

"Yup," I replied. "Well, actually I like all seasons. And I like them even better now that I live here in Stoneybrook."

"How come?"

"Because the seasons seem more real in the country. In New York they get sort of flattened out. Do you know what I mean? You can barely tell one from the other. In the autumn, you don't see the leaves change color unless you live near a park. In the winter, hardly any snow falls, and most of what does fall melts, because the city is so warm. Especially the streets and sidewalks."

"What with the subways and all," added Mal knowledgeably, even though she has been to New York, like, three times.

1

It was a Monday afternoon. Mal and I were walking home from school together. We go to Stoneybrook Middle School. Mal is in sixth grade and I am in eighth. (She's eleven and I'm thirteen.)

I am Stacey McGill. My parents named me Anastasia Elizabeth McGill, but they're the only ones who ever call me that — and when they do, I know I am in Deep Trouble. As you may have guessed, I used to live in New York City. In fact, I still go there pretty often. That's because my dad lives there. He and my mom are divorced now.

My recent life has been rife with drama. (I just love that phrase! I read it in a book.)

Maybe other kids have led more dramatic lives than I have, but mine has to be up there in the top twenty percent or so. (Which reminds me — I love math, too.) I am a native New Yorker. I was born in the city and I grew up there. My mom and dad and I lived in the same apartment until I was twelve. Then my dad's company transferred him to Connecticut, so we moved to Stoneybrook. I guess grown-ups aren't always too good at making up their minds, because after we'd lived in Stoneybrook for less than one year, Dad's boss transferred him back to New York. So we picked up and returned to the city — but to a different apartment.

Okay. I thought that was that. I had liked Stoneybrook all right, and I had loved my new school and especially my new friends, but I missed the city. I didn't mind returning. But I did mind that my parents started to fight. Not just a spat every now and then, but lots and lots of long, shouting arguments. Even so, I was taken by surprise when they told me they had decided to divorce. I thought that only happened to other families. Worse, Dad had decided to stay in the city (with his job), but Mom wanted to go back to Stoneybrook — and *I* had to choose which of them to live with. In the end I chose Mom, not because I love her more than Dad, but because I found myself missing Stoneybrook and needing my friends here.

Those things happened awhile ago. Now Mom and I are settled into a little old house which is directly in back of Mal's. And in the city, Dad is settled into a tiny two-bedroom apartment. (The second bedroom is mine, for when I visit my father.)

Mallory and I had reached her driveway, the spot where we usually separate. She follows the walk to her front door. I cut through her backyard and then mine, and enter my house through the kitchen.

"You're coming back at four, right?" Mal called over her shoulder.

"Yup. I'll see you then!"

Mal is the oldest of *eight* children. (Hers is the biggest family I have ever known.) I was going to help her baby-sit for her younger brothers and sisters for an hour, and then we were going to go to a meeting of the Baby-sitters Club together. (My friends and I call it the BSC. I'll tell you more about it later.)

I cut across the lawns and ran into my house. "Hi, Mom! I'm home!" I called. I headed for the refrigerator.

"Hi, honey." Mom entered the kitchen, looking pale and tired. She's been looking that way a lot lately. It comes from being a single parent who's job-hunting *and* doing temporary work.

"Wow," I said as Mom sank into a chair. "How many interviews did you go on today?"

"Two," she replied.

"Just two?" I would have guessed about ten.

"Just two. But I've lined up several more."

I nodded. "Mom, you don't have to rush, you know. I mean, about getting a job. Dad's paying alimony and child support . . . isn't he?"

"Oh, of course," Mom assured me. "But it isn't the same. Now his salary is paying for a house *and* an apartment. The money doesn't go as far these days. So I do need a job."

"Yeah." I was carefully putting together a

4

snack. I always have to plan my meals and snacks carefully. This is because I'm a diabetic. Diabetes is a disease in which this gland in your body, the pancreas, stops producing the proper amount of something called insulin. Your body needs insulin to break down sugar. If this system goes out of whack, you can get really sick. (Well, *I* can. I'm a brittle diabetic, which means I have a severe form of the disease.) Here's how I control my diabetes: by sticking to a strict no-sugar diet, and by giving myself injections of insulin. I know that's gross, but it has to be done.

"What are your plans this afternoon, honey?" Mom asked.

"I'm sitting at the Pikes' with Mal, but just for an hour. Then we're going to the BSC meeting. I'll be home by six-fifteen."

"Okay. Where's Dee going?" (Dee is Mrs. Pike, although that isn't her real first name. That's my mom's nickname for her. She and Mrs. Pike have gotten to be very close friends.)

"A school meeting," I replied. "The elementary school. Something about Claire's kindergarten class, I think."

"Mm." Mom nodded absently.

"Why don't you take a nap?" I suggested. "You look exhausted. I can start dinner. And I can finish it after the meeting. We can eat a little late tonight. I'll bring another snack to the meeting." (I also have to be careful about *when* I eat.)

"Well, I think I'll just take you up on your offer," said Mom.

"Good." The phone rang then, and I told Mom not to bother with it. Whatever it was, I would handle it. "Hello?" I said. I closed my eyes, allowing myself to wish that Sam Thomas would be on the other end of the line. Sam is my new friend. Who's a boy. I hesitate to call him my boyfriend, but, well, we date sometimes. Sam happens to be the older brother of Kristy Thomas, president of the Baby-sitters Club and one of my good friends. Sometimes this situation has been a bit awkward, but that never prevents me from hoping Sam will call.

"Hi, Stace! It's your old dad," said the caller cheerfully.

"Hi, Old Dad!" I replied. "You sound, um, perky."

"I have good news. Would you like to hear it?"

"Definitely."

"Your old dad has finally been promoted."

"Hey, great!" I cried.

"Nope," said Dad. "This is better than 'Hey, great.' This is major. I've been named vice-president of the company. I'm getting a raise,

6

a bigger office, the works. It's what I've been waiting for."

"Oh, my lord! Congratulations! Dad, that's fantastic!"

"Thank you, thank you. You can't see it, but I'm taking a bow." (I giggled.) "The company is even holding a dinner in my honor."

"Wow." That was impressive.

"I'd love for you to be there."

"Where? At the dinner?"

"Where else?"

"You mean kids can come?"

"Well, I don't think any other kids will be there. But you're special. You're the daughter of the man being honored. You can be my date."

"Cool. Okay. When is the dinner?" I was hoping Dad would say it was going to be on a Wednesday night or something, and then I could have a little break from school. But he didn't.

"It's a week from this coming Friday," he replied. "I thought you could stay in the city for the weekend. We'll make it special. I'll get tickets to something for Saturday night" — when Dad says "tickets to something" he means tickets to something on Broadway, like a play or a musical — "we'll eat at Tavern on the Green, go out for Sunday brunch, whatever you want. Oh, and why don't you buy yourself a new dress or outfit to wear to the dinner. Put it on a charge card. I'll pay your mother back."

"Awesome! Thanks, Dad! Listen, I have to go. I have a sitting job. But I'll tell Mom about the weekend, and I'll call you later so we can talk some more. Congratulations again!"

A few minutes later I was once more running through the yards, and then knocking breathlessly on the Pikes' back door.

Margo let me in. She's the seven-year-old Pike. Claire, the kindergartener, is the five-year-old. Then there are eight-year-old Nicky, nine-year-old Vanessa, and the ten-year-old triplets, Adam, Byron, and Jordan. (They're identical.)

"Hurry and come in!" exclaimed Margo, tugging at my hand. "Come see what we're doing. We are *very* busy."

Margo pulled me into the rec room where I found her brothers and sisters poring through magazines and comic books.

"What is this? A reading club?" I asked.

Jordan snorted. "A *read*ing club?"

"Jordan," said Mrs. Pike warningly.

"Sorry," said Jordan immediately.

Mrs. Pike looked at me apologetically. Then she said, "Mal, Stace — this should only take about an hour. I know you have a club meeting at five-thirty. I'll try to be back by five."

"Okay," Mal and I replied.

Mrs. Pike hurried through the door to the garage, and I approached Jordan. "So what *are* you doing?" I asked.

"Ordering stuff," he replied.

Vanessa looked up from a corner of the couch where she was sprawled, one magazine open in her hands, two others spread across her stomach. "You wouldn't be*lieve* what you can order," she said. "And cheaply. I already ordered a sample of hair conditioner. And a bust-developer. The bust-developer cost five dollars, almost, but the conditioner was practically free."

"Now we're going to see what else we can get for free," added Nicky.

"Here's something!" Adam called out triumphantly. "Well, it's almost free. For twenty-five cents you can order a trial pack of Ever-Flow baby bottle liners."

Mal and I exchanged a Look. Oh, well. At least the kids were busy. They entertained themselves until their mother returned.

CHAPTER 2

"EvenFlo baby bottle liners!" cried Mal.

"A *bust*-developer!" I crowed.

"I think my brothers and sisters are truly looney-tunes," added Mallory. "Every last one of them."

"How long have they been 'ordering stuff'?" I wanted to know.

"For about a week." Mal and I were pedaling our bikes to Claudia Kishi's house, where the BSC meeting would be held. "It started when Adam was looking through the back of one of his comic books and found an ad for something called 'fool's gold.' The ad said he could order his very own piece of fool's gold — in a quality felt pouch with a drawstring — for just fifty cents. So he did. And he and the other kids have been ordering things ever since. None of it has arrived yet, though."

We rode up Claud's driveway and chained

our bikes to the lamppost. Then we ran along the front walk and let ourselves inside. (All the BSC members do that. The Kishis don't mind.)

"Hello!" I called as we ran upstairs to Claudia's room.

"Hello!" Claud's voice drifted back to us. Claud is the vice-president of the BSC, I'm the treasurer, and Mallory is a junior officer.

Claudia Kishi is my very best friend in the entire world, and I am hers, even though we have only known each other since the beginning of seventh grade, when I moved to Stoneybrook for the first time. Like most best friends, Claud and I are practically twins in some ways, and true opposites in other ways. We are opposites in terms of our family situations and our looks. As you know, I have no brothers and sisters, and my parents are divorced. Claudia has an older sister (Janine the Genius) and her parents are happily married. Also, Claud has never moved. She was born in Stoneybrook and grew up in this house on Bradford Court. In terms of looks, I have fluffy blonde hair which my mom allows me to get permed, blue eyes, and I'm fairly thin, probably because of the diabetes. Claud, who is Japanese-American, has long, silky jet-black hair, and dark, almond-shaped eyes. Despite an addiction to junk food, she is not fat (or thin — she's just right) and she has a complexion like someone in the "after" part of a Clearasil ad.

But Claud and I have the exact same taste in clothes and fashion, and very similar interests. We are both sophisticated and trendy. I know I sound like I'm bragging, but everyone says this about us. We keep track of the new styles, and we wear tights and boots, baggy tops, and big jewelry. Claud likes hats, and often wears one, and we experiment with makeup and accessories. We experiment with our hair, too, especially Claudia.

Claud and I could talk about fashion and try on clothes endlessly, but we do have other interests — and those interests are another of our differences. While I enjoy school and especially like math, Claud can't stand school. She's an awful student and a terrible speller (although she's smart). What Claud likes is art. She's been taking art classes for years, and her room is full of evidence that she's a painter, a sketcher (is there such a word?), a potter, a sculptress, and a jewelry-maker. Claud makes lots of her own jewelry and often makes jewelry for her friends, too.

Let's see. Here's one other difference between Claud and me. Claud, as I mentioned, is addicted to junk food. Also to Nancy Drew mysteries. Since her parents don't approve of either habit, Claud ends up hiding stuff all over her room — candy, cookies, Ring-Dings, Ding-Dongs, mystery books. Of course, I can't eat most of the stuff Claudia craves, but she's nice about keeping pretzels or crackers on hand for me. Claud is always thoughtful.

"Hey, you guys!" called a voice.

"Hey!" replied Claud and Mal and I.

Standing in the doorway were Mary Anne Spier and Dawn Schafer, the secretary and alternate officer of the BSC. Guess what. They are best friends *and* stepsisters.

Like Claudia, Mary Anne grew up in Stoneybrook and for years she lived here on Bradford Court, across the street from Claud. She's an only child, and her mother died when Mary Anne was a baby, so until seventh grade, her family consisted of her and her father. Mr. Spier was extremely protective of Mary Anne, and also quite strict with her, but Mary Anne, although she's shy, managed to make a few good friends, including Kristy Thomas (her *first* best friend), who's the president of the BSC, and also Sam Thomas's sister (remember?). Then, when Dawn Schafer moved to Stoneybrook from California after her parents got divorced, Mary Anne became friends with Dawn, too. In fact, Dawn soon became her *other* best friend. *Then* (and this is the good part) Dawn and Mary Anne decided to fix up

Mrs. Schafer and Mr. Spier. After their parents dated for what seemed like forever . . . they got married! That's how the best friends became stepsisters. So Mary Anne finally had what she thought of as a "real family." (In my opinion, *one* person can be a family just as nicely as a mom and a dad, two kids, a cat, and a dog.)

Anyway, Mary Anne seems happier now and a little less shy. And her dad is a little less strict. But Mary Anne is still quiet. Plus, she's romantic, and she cries at the drop of a hat. Mary Anne was the first one of us BSC members to wind up with a steady boyfriend. His name is Logan Bruno, and he's one of the nicest guys I know. He and Mary Anne are perfect for each other, although they have had their ups and downs (like most couples, I guess).

Mary Anne has brown eyes and shoulder-length brown hair, and she's short, one of the shortest girls in our class. (Kristy is *the* shortest, though.) Thanks to her father, Mary Anne used to have to dress like a first-grader and wear her hair in braids. Now she's allowed to dress more the way she wants (which is tame compared to Claud and me), and to let her hair down. She is not, however, allowed to get her ears pierced. Every other member of the BSC, except for Kristy, has pierced ears.

Claud even has *double*-pierced ears, while Dawn has two holes in one ear and one hole in the other. Oh, well. Mary Anne can still wear earrings. Claud makes clip-ons for her.

Dawn is pretty different from Mary Anne. For instance, she comes from a *very* different family. She was born in California and lived there with her parents and her younger brother Jeff until the divorce. (Jeff still lives in California with his father.) After the divorce, Dawn made the adjustment from her warm, sunny home state to cold, snowy Connecticut. (Dawn moved here in the middle of winter.) Now her new family — Dawn, her mom, Mary Anne, Mary Anne's dad, and Tigger, Mary Anne's gray tiger kitten — lives in the farmhouse Mrs. Schafer (now Mrs. Spier) bought. Dawn loves the farmhouse. It is old and quirky, has a secret passage which was once part of the Underground Railroad, and may even be haunted by a ghost. This is perfect for Dawn who adores mysteries and ghost stories.

I admire Dawn for two reasons. One, her recent life has been tough like mine (rife with drama), but she's pulled through just fine. Two, Dawn is an individual, and not afraid to stand up for the things in which she believes, even if her beliefs set her apart from others. She won't compromise; she stands firm.

15

Maybe this is why other kids like Dawn, too. She has a lot of admirers (but no steady boyfriend).

Dawn looks nothing at all like Mary Anne. Nobody would ever mistake them for natural sisters. She has LONG blonde hair, even longer than Claud's, and it is much lighter than mine. It's so blonde it's almost white. Her eyes are blue, and her nose and cheeks are sprinkled with freckles. Dawn is thin, probably because of her eating habits, which are as different from Claud's as night and day. Dawn sticks to an extremely healthy diet, not because she has to but because she wants to. She won't touch red meat, and she keeps her distance from junk food, especially sugar. (Yea, Dawn!) As for Dawn's clothes, my friends and I call her style California casual. (We made up that term.) It means that she likes to look trendy, but to be comfortable and individualistic at the same time. What else would you expect from Dawn?

The next two people to arrive at Claud's were Jessi Ramsey and Kristy Thomas. They didn't arrive together, though, because Kristy lives in a different neighborhood from the rest of us. Jessi (short for Jessica) is Mallory's best friend. Jessi and Mal are both junior members of the BSC, since they are eleven and the rest of us are thirteen. Here is something interesting: Jessi lives in my old house, the one I lived in the first time I moved to Stoneybrook. When my family left, Jessi's moved in. The Ramseys came to Stoneybrook at the beginning of this school year when Mr. Ramsey's company transferred him. Jessi's family consists of Jessi, her parents, her Aunt Cecelia, her younger sister Becca (short for Rebecca), her baby brother Squirt (whose real name is John Philip Ramsey, Jr.), and their hamster Misty. (You already know most of who's in Mal's family — her parents, a hamster named Frodo, and those eight kids!)

Although Jessi and Mal are similar in that they're both the oldest kids in their families *and* feel that their parents treat them like infants anyway, their main interests are fairly different. They enjoy reading, especially horse stories, but Mal hopes to write and illustrate children's books one day, while Jessi dreams of being a professional ballerina. Actually, Jessi is well on her way. I'm pretty sure her dream is going to come true. Jessi has taken dance for years and now dances *en pointe.* (That means "on toe.") When she moved to Connecticut she was even accepted at a special dance school in Stamford, which is the nearest big city. She takes classes there in the afternoons and has already danced the lead in several of her school productions. I really admire Jessi's talent and determination.

Like Mary Anne and Dawn, Jessi and Mal are another pair of best friends who look nothing alike. Jessi is black with deep brown eyes, and usually wears her hair up or pulled back for dance class. Mal is white with red hair, blue eyes, and freckles, and wears glasses and braces. Even though the braces are the clear kind that hardly show up, Mal doesn't feel very pretty and wishes desperately for contact lenses. Her parents say no, though. They also say no to most of the trendy clothes she wants to wear. (So do Jessi's parents.) Mal and Jessi are lucky to get by looking like sixth-graders, let alone fashion plates.

Finally, let me introduce you to Kristy Thomas, BSC president, creator, and founder. I think Kristy has the most interesting and unusual family of any of us, although it didn't start out that way. The Thomases began as a nice, regular family — mother, father, Kristy, and her three brothers. Kristy's brothers are Sam (of course) who is fifteen, Charlie who's seventeen, and David Michael who's seven. Shortly after David Michael was born, Mr. Thomas walked out on the family, leaving Kristy's mom to raise the kids by herself. She did a great job, managing to keep the house on Bradford Court (Kristy used to live next door to Mary Anne) and to hold her family together. Then, when Kristy was in seventh grade, her mother met and fell in love with a man named Watson Brewer. By the summer, they had gotten married and Watson, who's a millionaire, had moved the Thomases across town into his mansion. That was when Kristy's family began to change. Watson became her stepfather, and his children from his first marriage (Karen who's seven and Andrew who's four) became her stepsister and stepbrother. Then her mom and Watson adopted a little girl from Vietnam. Her name is Emily Michelle and she's two and a half. To help care for Emily, Kristy's grandmother moved in. And to round out the family are the pets — Shannon, David Michael's puppy; Boo-Boo, Watson's cat; and two goldfish belonging to Karen and Andrew. What a household!

Kristy Thomas is a real character. She is outgoing, outspoken, and full of energy and ideas. Pretty different from Mary Anne, her only best friend, except for looks. Kristy and Mary Anne could pass for sisters, but they sure don't dress alike. Kristy, who loves sports, dresses for comfort alone; almost always in jeans, a turtleneck shirt, sneakers, and maybe a sweat shirt and a baseball cap.

Kristy likes sports and children so much that

she combined the two interests and started a softball team for little kids. The team is called Kristy's Krushers. Through coaching, Kristy met the coach of a rival team, Bart's Bashers. Now she and Bart Taylor go out sometimes, but Kristy would probably kill me if she heard me refer to Bart as her boyfriend.

Kristy's big ideas are what led to the creation of the BSC. The members of the Baby-sitters Club, which is really a business, meet three times a week, on Monday, Wednesday, and Friday afternoons from five-thirty until six. Because we advertise, parents know they can reach us at those times, so they call then to line up sitters for their kids. Kristy came up with the idea for the club when she realized how hard her mother sometimes had to look to find a sitter for David Michael (if Kristy or Sam or Charlie couldn't watch him). Her mother would have a much easier job if she could make one phone call and reach a whole bunch of available sitters. One of them would certainly be free to take the job. That's what our club does, and it runs smoothly and efficiently. As president, Kristy sees to that. Claudia, vice-president, lends us her room, her phone (she has a private line), and her hidden snacks three times a week. Mary Anne schedules our sitting jobs in the club record book and also keeps up-to-date the information we store there: our clients' names, addresses, and phone numbers, the rates they pay, and so forth. As treasurer, I collect dues from the members each Monday and dole it out as needed — for instance, we pay Charlie Thomas to drive Kristy to and from meetings, and help Claud with her phone bill. Dawn's job, as alternate officer, is to take over the duties of anyone who can't make a meeting. And Jessi and Mal . . . well, they don't have actual duties. Junior officer means they can't sit at night, unless they're watching their own brothers and sisters, but they take on a lot of the daytime jobs, which frees us older members for the evening jobs.

To help the club work even more effectively, Kristy came up with three more great ideas. One was the club notebook in which each club member must write up every sitting job she goes on. Then the rest of us are responsible for reading it once a week. This is a good way to keep up with the lives of the children we care for, and to find out how our friends handled sitting problems. The second idea was Kid-Kits. She invented the idea of decorating an ordinary cardboard carton and filling it with her old games, books, and toys, plus some new things such as art supplies, and bringing it with her on sitting jobs. Now we each have a Kid-Kit — and we have become very popular

21

sitters! The third idea was to sign up two extra club members as associates. The associate members don't attend meetings. They're reliable sitters we can call on if a job happens to come along that none of us is available to take. That doesn't happen often, but when it does, we're extremely grateful for Shannon Kilbourne (a friend of Kristy's who lives in her new neighborhood) and Logan Bruno who is . . . Mary Anne's boyfriend!

Kristy seated herself in Claud's director's chair, adjusted her visor, and kept her eyes on the digital clock, our official club timepiece. When the numbers changed from 5:29 to 5:30, Kristy rapped a pencil on the arm of the chair and announced, "This meeting of the Baby-sitters Club will now come to order. Will the treasurer please collect the weekly dues?" Kristy turned her attention to me.

Grudgingly, everyone handed me a dollar, which I dropped into the BSC treasury (a manila envelope). I was dumping out the contents of the envelope so I could count the money, when the phone rang. Our first job call of the day. Jessi lunged for it.

"Hi, Mrs. Barrett!" she said a moment later. "Sunday? I'll call you right back."

Mrs. Barrett, a regular client of the BSC, lives near the Pikes and has three children.

Mary Anne checked the appointment pages in the record book and scheduled Dawn for the job. Then Jessi called Mrs. Barrett back to tell her who'd be sitting for Buddy, Suzi, and Marnie.

After that, I finished counting the treasury money and we answered a few more calls. Finally things calmed down. During a moment of silence, Mal said, "Guess what the latest project at my house is?" Then she told everyone about the mail-order craze.

Dawn began to laugh. "You know what I did once? I found this great offer in a magazine. For a dollar forty-nine I got twelve cassettes."

"Twelve!" exclaimed Jessi.

"Yeah. But I didn't realize that by doing that, I'd joined a cassette *club*. Every month another cassette arrived in the mail and I was supposed to pay almost full price for each one. I never had enough money. Finally I had to ask Dad to get me out of the club."

"Once," began Kristy, "I saw this ad on TV. The announcer said you could order this great collection of fifties and sixties rock 'n' roll songs by the original artists. You know what happened? The cassette arrived, but it turned out to be a collection of the old songs performed by a new group called the Original Artists. What a rip-off! I thought I was going to be hearing music by the Drifters, Buddy Holly, the Chiffons, and Gladys Knight and the Pips."

"I can't wait to see what's going to start arriving at my house," said Mal. "My brothers and sisters may be surprised."

The phone rang then and we scheduled a job for Mary Anne with the Kuhn kids. Then we scheduled another job. In the lull that followed, I said, "Well, I have some news."

"Good news?" Claud wanted to know.

"Yup. My dad called this afternoon. He's being given a huge raise and a promotion in his company. He's going to become a vice-president. And his company is honoring him with a dinner."

"Awesome," said Dawn.

"I know. I can tell Dad is really pleased. *And* he invited me to come to New York and be his date at the dinner. It's a week from Friday. I'm going to spend the weekend in the city. Dad's getting tickets to a play and everything. Oh, and he told me to buy a new outfit."

"That's fantastic!" exclaimed Claud, "Hey, let's celebrate. Let's go shopping on Saturday. We'll all come with you, Stace, and help you choose an outfit, and then we can eat downtown."

"We could go to that new place," added Mary Anne.

"Ye Olde Ice-Cream Parlour?" said Kristy. (She pronounced "olde" like this: oldie.)

Mary Anne giggled. "Well, it looks like ye 'oldie' ice-cream parlour, but I think it's called the Rosebud Cafe. And it serves more than just ice cream."

"Whatever it's called, let's go there," said Claud. "I peeked in the windows the other day and the ice cream and sundaes look amazing."

"Sounds great," I replied, even though I would have to celebrate with a boring old diet soda. "Can everybody go?"

"Yes!" said Claud, Kristy, Mary Anne, and Dawn.

But Jessi shook her head. "Special dance class."

And Mal, looking pained, said, "Visiting my grandparents for the day. You guys better go anyway, though. You don't have much time to get a new outfit, Stace. You can't waste Saturday."

Which was how our Saturday shopping excursion and celebration was planned.

CHAPTER 3

On Saturday morning I slept late and woke up leisurely, which is the perfect way to start any weekend. I reached for my clock radio and turned it toward me. Five minutes to nine.

"Morning, Mom," I mumbled as I groped my way into the kitchen.

"Morning," she replied.

I sat at the table, surprised to see only my place set. "Did you already eat?" I asked.

My mother shook her head. "I'm not hungry this morning, but I'll fix you something. What do you want?"

I ate toast and fruit, and Mom and I talked about the weekend. At nine-thirty I said, "Whoa, I better get dressed. Mary Anne and Dawn are going to be here soon."

Before I knew it, Mr. Spier had pulled up in front of my house and I was clambering into the backseat of his car with my friends. Ten minutes later, we were being dropped off outside Bellair's Department Store. Kristy was waiting for us. Dressed in jeans, a bulky red sweat shirt, and sneakers, she was sitting on a bench, reading a copy of *Sports Illustrated*.

"Hi, you guys!" she called. "Charlie dropped me off early. Where's Claud?"

"On her way, I guess," I replied. "Her mom has to work today. She was going to drop Claud here before she went to the library." (Mrs. Kishi is the head librarian at the Stoneybrook Public Library.)

At that moment a horn honked. Mrs. Kishi, who was slowing to a stop, waved to Mr. Spier as he pulled into the traffic. And Claud scrambled out of her mom's car.

"We're all here!" she exclaimed. "Okay, let's hit the stores. 'Bye, Mom!"

Kristy waited until both Mrs. Kishi and Mr. Spier had disappeared from view. Then she said, "Ah. Parent-free."

We invaded Bellair's first.

"Which department?" asked Mary Anne.

"Dresses," I replied.

Kristy groaned.

"Well, where do *you* want to go?" asked Claud.

"Sports."

"To look for a dress for Stacey?"

"No, to look for a new baseball cap for me."

"Let's look for Stacey's outfit first. That's the most important thing today. The dinner is in less than a week."

We rode the elevator to the second floor, Kristy bringing up the rear. But before we were halfway to Junior Dresses, we passed a jewelry counter. Not costume jewelry, fine jewelry.

Claud stopped. She leaned over and peered at a necklace displayed on a swatch of blue velvet. "Oh, my lord," she whispered.

"What?" replied Dawn, turning around.

Claud pointed at the counter. "Guess how much that necklace costs," she managed to say. She was still whispering.

We all leaned in for a look.

"What's it made of?" asked Dawn.

"Sapphires and diamonds, I think."

"Sapphires and diamonds? Four hundred dollars?" guessed Dawn.

"Four *hun*dred?" Try a thousand," said Kristy.

"Try *four* thousand," said Claud. "It costs *four thousand* dollars."

"You could buy a *car* for four thousand dollars," I exclaimed. "Couldn't you? . . . Well, maybe not," I answered my own question. "But still . . ."

We had spread out and were gazing at the other jewelry on display.

"Here's a cheap pin. Just six hundred dollars," I said, giggling.

"Are you interested in it?"

I found myself looking into the humorless eyes of a salesclerk. "Um, no," I answered. "Thanks anyway. Come on, you guys."

We dragged ourselves away from the jewelry and finally (after stopping to look at hair accessories and knee socks) wound up in Junior Dresses.

"Here's a nice one," said Mary Anne. She held out a plaid dress that maybe a grandmother would look okay in, but not me.

I shook my head.

Dawn pointed to a floral-print dress.

I shook my head. "I need something wild."

"Not too wild," Mary Anne cautioned. "Not for a dinner with your dad."

"I'll find something," I said confidently.

We wandered through Bellair's for nearly an hour. Claud bought a pair of black-and-white checked leggings. Mary Anne bought a hair ribbon. Kristy made fun of a two-thousand-dollar brooch.

"Where now?" asked Dawn as we were leaving the store.

"The Merry-Go-Round," I replied.

"They don't sell clothes."

"I know. I want to look at the jewelry."

So we wandered around in the Merry-Go-

Round for awhile. Dawn bought a pair of fat silver hoop earrings. I bought a pair of dangly blue shell earrings. Kristy said, "I forgot to look at the baseball caps!"

"Now where to?" asked Dawn.

"Maybe we should have asked someone to drive us out to Washington Mall," said Mary Anne. "It has a lot more stores to choose from."

"Yeah," I answered. "But not . . . Zingy's."

"Zingy's! That's all punk stuff. You won't find anything in there for a fancy dinner with the people in your father's company," said Mary Anne.

Claud grinned at me. "She might," she said.

"I like to think of myself as the Sherlock Holmes of fashion," I added. "No problem too tough to solve. I'll put together the perfect outfit at Zingy's. Trust me. It'll be perfect for me *and* my dad."

In all honesty, I didn't expect to find quite such a challenge at Zingy's. Putting together the perfect outfit there took a little longer than I'd planned. But I did it. (I think I drove the saleswoman crazy in the process, though.) By the time I left I was carrying a shopping bag in which were folded a hot pink (fake) silk jacket which fell to my knees, new black leggings, pink-and-black socks, and a black body suit. I planned to wear the outfit with black flats, and to dress it up with some jewelry and maybe a couple of barrettes in my hair.

When Claud saw me in the final combination of clothes (standing next to a chair piled high with discarded jackets, pants, tops, and socks), she drew in her breath. "You look fabulous. It *is* the perfect outfit," she said.

Twenty minutes later we were leaving Zingy's. I was lugging the shopping bag, Claud was carrying a bag full of cloth headbands, Dawn was carrying another pair of earrings, and Mary Anne was carrying a package of scented pens which had been on display near the cash register. Kristy had bought nothing. "Zingy's doesn't carry baseball caps," she complained.

I think we were glad to sit down when we reached the Rosebud Cafe. We chose a round table in a corner, dropped our packages to the floor, and sank into our chairs.

"I wonder why shopping is so tiring," said Kristy. "It's not as if you spend a lot of energy standing around looking at racks of clothes."

"It's mental energy," I told her. "All that planning and price comparing."

"I guess . . ." Kristy trailed off. Something had caught her attention. "Hey!" she exclaimed. "Look at the front of the restaurant! There's a real soda fountain, like from the olden days. Let's sit at the counter."

Suddenly we didn't feel so tired. We picked up our bags and moved to the counter. Then we sat on the tall stools and pretended we were college students in the 1940s. We ate salads and burgers, and then splurged on dessert. (Well, Kristy and Claud and Mary Anne splurged. Dawn settled for some carrot juice thing and I ordered a second diet Coke.)

Claud raised her ice-cream cone in the air. "Here's to your dad," she said.

"Here's to New York," said Mary Anne, who would like to live there.

"Here's to a great weekend," I added.

When Mr. Spier dropped me at my house that afternoon, I ran inside with my purchases. "Mom!" I called.

"In here, honey."

I found my mother lying on the couch in the living room. "What's wrong?" I asked, alarmed.

Mom coughed. "Just tired. I needed a little rest." She propped herself up on one elbow. "What did you buy? You look like you had success."

"Yup. Want a fashion show?"

"Of course."

"Okay. This'll take a few minutes." I dashed upstairs with the bag from Zingy's and carefully put on the entire outfit. I even added some jewelry and pulled my hair back with barrettes. Then I walked slowly down the stairs, trying to look like a fashion model, waltzed into the living room, and executed a turn.

Mom smiled. "Ravishing," she said.

"Honest? And do you really think this is all right for an important dinner with, like, Dad's boss and everyone? I mean, it *did* come from Zingy's."

"You look lovely, honey. Sophisticated and beautiful."

"Thanks."

Mom lay back against the pillows then, which surprised me because I had thought she was going to get up. "What did you *do* today?" I asked. Maybe she had gone out with one of her friends.

"Cleaned a little," said Mom, coughing again. "Oh! I almost forgot. Someone from Bellair's called this morning about the buyer's job. Remember? The one I interviewed for?" (I nodded.) "Well, she asked me to come in for a second interview. We scheduled it for Wednesday."

"Hey, that's great! Isn't it?"

"It means she's interested enough to want to talk to me again."

"Cool! . . . Hey, Mom, if you got a job with Bellair's would we get a discount at the store?"

Mom smiled wryly. "Probably."

"Oh, puh-*lease* do well at the interview!"

"I'll try my best."

"Thank you, thank you, thank you. I now volunteer to make dinner again."

"I now accept again."

"Take another nap," I suggested.

"Yes, ma'am." Mom dutifully closed her eyes.

I returned to my room. Before I thought about dinner, I took another look in the mirror. I imagined myself at the fancy dinner, sitting next to my father. The weekend was going to be wonderful. I just knew it. I could hardly wait for my trip to the Big Apple.

CHAPTER 4

Sunday

Mal, your brothers and sisters aren't the only ones who are ordering stuff from magazines. Every kid in the neighborhood is doing it. I sat for the Barretts this afternoon, and Buddy was already filling out forms when I came over. After awhile Matt and Haley Braddock stopped by, and then Jake Kuhn did, and finally Nicky and Vanessa. Each of them was armed with magazines and comic books, and Haley even brought along her return address labels to cut down on the number of times she'd have to write out her name and address.

You guys, you should see what the kids are ordering.

The day after our trip downtown to buy my new outfit and to celebrate Dad's promotion, Dawn baby-sat for Buddy, Suzi, and Marnie Barrett. She sits for them pretty often. They live nearby and are regular clients of the BSC. Mr. and Mrs. Barrett were divorced recently, which has been hard on the kids, but this may be one reason they get along well with Dawn. Since *she* has just been through a divorce, she can sympathize with them. She talks to them and answers their questions honestly.

On Sunday, though, the divorce was the farthest thing from the minds of the Barretts. They were much too busy filling out forms and addressing envelopes. At least, the older kids were. Marnie, the youngest (she's just two), was busy with a box of Kleenex. (The things that will entertain kids amaze me sometimes.) But Buddy who's eight and Suzi who's five were thoroughly engrossed in a stack of copies of *Good Housekeeping*, *Ladies' Home Journal*, and Dawn wasn't sure what else. Suzi can't write yet, so she couldn't fill out forms, but she adored looking through the magazines, and Buddy instructed her to lick stamps and seal envelopes.

When Mrs. Barrett had left the house Dawn, carrying Marnie on one hip, entered the rec room where Buddy and Suzi had set up shop.

"This place looks like an office!" exclaimed Dawn.

Buddy beamed. "I guess it is sort of an office."

He and Suzi were sitting on the floor. Around them were spread scissors, pencils, envelopes, stamps, tape, and even some money.

Suzi saw Dawn glance at the money. "Mommy gave us that," she said happily. "She told us we could order whatever we want."

"And we added our own money to it," said Buddy.

"How much did you say we have altogether?" asked Suzi.

"Well, we *had* twelve dollars and sixty cents, but now we have used up some of it. So we have to order really cheap things."

"Okay," said Suzi uncertainly. Then she held a magazine toward her brother. "Buddy? Is this cheap?"

"The ring?" Buddy squinted at the page. "No. It costs almost fifteen dollars. I wish you could read, Suzi."

"Me, too."

Dawn began to look through the small pile of envelopes that Buddy had declared were ready to mail. "What have you ordered so far?" she asked.

"A needle-threader!" exclaimed Suzi. "I found that. What did the ad say, Buddy? I don't remember."

"It said 'You never need thread a needle again. Amazing Seamstress Helper does it for you.' We thought Mom should have that."

"I didn't know your mom likes to sew," said Dawn.

"She . . . well, she might," Suzi replied.

"Anyway the Seamstress Helper only cost a dollar twenty-nine," said Buddy.

"And then we found special silver polish," Suzi went on.

"No-tarnish silver polish," Buddy explained. "The hostess's best friend."

"And I don't remember how much it cost, but we sent away for a book for Marnie," said Suzi. "A very personal book."

"A personal*ized* book," her brother corrected her. "It is so cool, Dawn. You just fill out some information like Marnie's name and her age, and — boom — they send you a story about a two-year-old girl named Marnie. She is going to love — Oh! Oh, wow! I *have* to have this!" Buddy had continued to pore through the magazines while he was talking to Dawn, but now he had stopped and was jabbing excitedly at a page.

"What did you find?" asked Dawn, peering over his shoulder.

"A book. A book for me! It's called *How to Become Mr. Muscle!*"

"You want to be a strongman?"

"I want to look like Arnold Schwarzenegger. That would be way cool."

"Who's Arnie Swarteneggy?" asked Suzi.

"A movie star. Everyone likes him."

Buddy was frantically cutting the order blank out of the magazine when the Barretts' bell rang.

"I'll get it!" cried Suzi.

"Make sure you know who's at the door before you let them in," Dawn cautioned her. "Look out the window first."

Suzi disappeared up the stairs to the first floor. Buddy filled out the form. And Dawn cried, "Don't *eat* the Kleenex, Marnie!"

"Once," said Buddy absently, "Marnie ate so much Kleenex she threw up."

"Ew," replied Dawn, and was saved from a disgusting conversation when Suzi returned to the rec room with Matt and Haley Braddock, who live in the neighborhood. Haley is nine and Matt is seven. Matt and Buddy are good friends, but they usually need Haley around when they get together. This is because Matt is deaf and communicates using sign language. Buddy (and most of the kids who spend time with Matt) know some sign language, but not enough for long or complicated conversations.

Matt and Haley bounced into the rec room carrying armloads of comic books, a supply of envelopes, and Haley's address labels.

"We found wart-remover this morning!" Haley announced, at the same time signing, for Matt's benefit.

"You guys have warts?" asked Dawn, removing a hunk of Kleenex from Marnie's fist.

"No, but I bet someone we know does."

"Hey!" exclaimed Buddy. "Here's a simple kitchen tool that allows you to make your own garnishes for gourmet meals."

"How much?" asked Haley.

"Two ninety-five. You can make radish rosebuds and all sorts of things." Buddy filled out the order form.

When Jake Kuhn arrived with *his* comic books he said, "I found a kit that lets you grow your own catnip!"

"When did you get a cat?" asked Dawn.

"Well, we didn't. But . . . hey, Mary Anne has a cat, doesn't she?"

"Yes," agreed Dawn, hiding a smile.

"Ooh, pumpkin seeds!" exclaimed Suzi as the bell rang again.

Nicky and Vanessa had arrived. They strutted into the rec room, looking important. "Guess what came in the mail yesterday," said Nicky.

All heads turned toward him.

"Something *came*?" said Jake, awed.

Nicky nodded. "I got the mail myself, and when I opened our box, I saw a big envelope. *My* name was on it. It is so, so cool to get mail. I opened the envelope, and inside was . . . a tube of stain remover."

"I got something, too," Vanessa spoke up. "Freckle-remover. I used it last night before I went to bed. Do I look any different?"

Haley leaned over and studied Vanessa's nose. "I think your freckles are paler," she said.

Vanessa nodded. "In two weeks they should have faded completely. They will vanish from my face. I can't wait."

"Lucky ducks," said Jake. "None of my stuff has come yet."

"Mine either," added Buddy. "Maybe tomorrow."

"Really?" shrieked Suzi. "Really? I might get mail tomorrow?"

"You *all* might," Dawn told her. "You guys will be getting mail for days."

"Awesome," said Buddy, and returned to his magazine.

CHAPTER 5

This is how much I like math. I don't even mind math tests. I don't even mind *studying* for math tests. On Monday my class took a V.I.T. (Very Important Test). It was one of the ones that counts for, like, a fifth of your report card grade.

I had studied hard on Sunday and I knew the material. Our current unit is pre-algebra. To me, figuring out what x and y equal is like solving a mystery. (I wish I could convince Claudia to think of math that way, but she won't do it. Once I even told her to call herself a Math Detective, but she just looked at me like I'd lost my mind.)

I concentrated on my test paper. $X = 3Y + 4$. If y equals . . .

"Mr. Zizmore? Mr. Zizmore?" The school secretary was calling my teacher over the PA system. It crackled loudly.

I jumped a mile, and my hand jerked off the paper, leaving a pencil trail.

"Yes?" replied Mr. Zizmore importantly.

"Is Stacey McGill in class?"

"Yes," he said again. He turned to look at me, and so did every student in the room. They were curious. Also, they were glad for the interruption in their test-taking. I heard sighs, knuckles cracking, feet shuffling.

"Would you ask her to come to the office, please?"

"I'll send her at the end of the period," Mr. Zizmore replied. "She's in the middle of a test."

"No, it's important. Please ask her to come now, and tell her to stop by her locker on the way and pick up her coat."

"Okay." Mr. Zizmore turned to me again. "Did you hear that, Stacey?"

I nodded, confused. I'd been concentrating hard on the math problems, and now, suddenly, I was told to abandon them and report to the office — with my coat, which could only mean I was leaving school.

Feeling the eyes of my classmates follow me to Mr. Zizmore's desk, I handed him my paper. "It's only half-finished," I said.

He smiled. "Don't worry. You're a good student. We'll straighten this out tomorrow." He paused. "I hope everything's all right."

"Thanks," I replied. Then I dashed out of the room, ran to my locker, grabbed a few things from it, and hurried on to the office.

Mrs. Downey, one of the secretaries, was waiting for me. "Hi, Stacey," she said as soon as I appeared. She led me into an empty office.

"What's wrong? Something is wrong, isn't it?" I cried.

"Your mother — " Mrs. Downey began to say.

"My mother? What about my mother?"

"She collapsed a little while ago. She was at a job interview at a company downtown and she just — collapsed."

Fell over? Fell down? Fainted? What?

"Where is she now?" I demanded.

"At the hospital, hon," said Mrs. Downey. "Mrs. Pike phoned. Mallory Pike's mother. She said she's a good friend of *your* mother?" (I nodded.) "Okay. She's on her way over here to pick you up. Then she'll drive you to the hospital. Do you have all your things with you?"

"Yes," I whispered.

"Good. Take a seat on the bench by the door. Mrs. Pike should be here any minute. I'll get you a glass of water."

I sat on the bench clutching my coat and wondering why people hand out glasses of water during a crisis. I didn't even notice the

44

stares of the kids who passed by in the hall.

When Mrs. Pike arrived, I jumped up and ran out of the office without bothering to greet her. Halfway down the hallway, I called, "Where are you parked?" and kept on hurrying.

"By the front door, sweetie," Mrs. Pike replied. "Stace, it's okay. Your mother is going to be okay."

"But Mrs. Downey said she collapsed."

"I know. The doctors will take care of her, though."

Maybe. But doctors are not magic. I know that.

Mrs. Pike drove to the hospital as fast as she could without getting arrested. She managed to find a parking space and we rushed inside, following signs to the admittance desk.

"Where's my mother?" I asked breathlessly, leaning over the desk. "She was just brought in. Her name is Mrs. McGill. I don't even know what's wrong with her."

The man behind the desk pointed down the hallway. "She's still in the emergency room, but — "

"They'll let me see her, won't they? I'm her daugher."

"Go ahead," said the man.

Mom was lying on a gurney (I know terms like that because of the unfortunate amount of time I myself have spent as a hospital patient) in a tiny room off the waiting area near the emergency entrance.

She was by herself.

"Mom?" I whispered. Her eyes were closed, so I didn't know if she was asleep or just resting or what.

She opened them slowly. "Hi, honey."

"Mom, what happened? Are you hurt?"

My mother shook her head slightly. "No, but I feel *awful*." She coughed.

I put my hand on her forehead. "Hey, you're burning up!"

"I know."

"Is it the flu or something? You know flu season is here. Mom, did you ever get your flu shot? You made me get one."

"I don't think this is the flu, Stacey."

"Where are the doctors?" I demanded. "Why are you here alone?"

"Doctors and nurses have been coming and going," Mom told me. She glanced up and noticed Mrs. Pike standing in the doorway. "Hi, Dee," she said weakly. She sounded like she might cry. "Thank you for bringing Stacey here. I appreciate it."

Mrs. Pike smiled. Then she stepped into the room and clasped Mom's hand.

"What do the doctors say, Mom?" I wanted to know.

She shook her head. "They aren't sure yet. They've taken a chest X-ray and drawn blood and examined every inch of me."

"Oh." A horrible thought occurred to me then. I remembered this girl who went to my old school in New York. One day she had a sore throat and a fever. Her parents took her to the doctor. They thought she had a strep throat. It turned out that she had leukemia. Cancer.

What if Mom had leukemia? What if she got really, really sick and I had to leave Stoneybrook and move in with my dad? What if —

"Mrs. McGill?" A doctor bustled into the room carrying a clipboard. She shooed Mrs. Pike and me into the hallway.

When she called us back a little while later, Mom was smiling thinly at us from the gurney. "Pneumonia," she said. "I have pneumonia."

"The good news is that she can be cared for at home," the doctor spoke up. "She doesn't need to be admitted to the hospital."

"What's the bad news?" I asked.

"That I have pneumonia, Stace!" exclaimed Mom. "Now come on. Let's get out of here. I'd like to be in my own bed as soon as possible."

Mrs. Pike drove Mom and me home. As she pulled into our driveway I thought to ask, "Hey, Mom? Where's *our* car?"

"Downtown. It's parked near Bellair's."

"Mr. Pike will drive it back tonight, Stacey," said Mal's mother. "Don't worry. Let's just take care of your mom now."

We helped Mom up the stairs, into her room, into her nightgown, and into her bed. "Ahh," she said. "I think I could sleep for a century." She promptly closed her eyes.

Mrs. Pike and I tiptoed back downstairs. "I'll get these prescriptions filled," she said. "Will you be okay here with your mom?"

"Oh, sure. I'm a great nurse," I said confidently. "Remember, I've had plenty of experience being a patient."

Not long after Mrs. Pike left, the phone calls began.

"Stace, where *were* you?" Kristy wanted to know.

"You aren't sick again, are you?" asked Claud.

"We waited for you after school," said Mary Anne.

My friends called separately, so I had to tell the same story over and over (except to Mallory, who heard it from her mother). If I'd been able to go to the BSC meeting I could have gotten away with telling it just once. But of course I didn't attend the meeting. Dawn took over my duties and collected dues.

Near dinnertime I was in the kitchen, busy making chicken noodle soup (oh, all right — heating up canned soup), when Claud called back. "How's your mom?" she wanted to know. "Everyone was asking about her at the meeting."

"Okay, I guess. She's just sleeping mostly. She wakes up long enough to take her pills, then she drifts off. I hope she'll eat something tonight, but I don't know."

"Will you be in school tomorrow?" asked Claud.

"I — Oh, I hear my mom! She's awake after all. Claud, I better go. I have to see how she is. Call you later. 'Bye."

It was while I was on the phone again with Claudia later in the evening that something occurred to me. If I didn't even know whether I'd be in school the next day, what was I going to do about the weekend? My big weekend in the Big Apple was supposed to begin in four days. What on earth was I going to do about it?

CHAPTER 6

I did not sleep much Monday night. I kept listening for Mom. She was coughing a lot. And twice I had to wake her up to give her pills. Each time I returned to my bed, I just lay there, one ear trained in the direction of my mother's room. No wonder new parents don't get much sleep, I thought. When they aren't up feeding the baby, they're probably lying awake listening for the sound of crying.

Around five-thirty on Tuesday morning I finally gave up on the idea of sleep. I tiptoed out of my room and peeked in at my mother. I thought she sounded a little better. She had not coughed in almost half an hour. I settled myself into a chair just outside Mom's room and began to read.

"Stacey?" called Mom.

It was after seven. I was halfway finished with the book.

I jumped up and ran to her bed. "Good morning," I said cheerfully.

"Morning." (Cough, cough.) "Shouldn't you be getting ready for school?"

"Me? No, I'm staying home today." (I had made that decision at three-thirty, lying awake in my bed.)

"But it's Tuesday . . . isn't it?"

"Yes. And you're sick."

"It isn't necessary for you to stay home with me, though."

"Mom. I'm not leaving you. You have pneu*m*onia."

"Honey, Dee will drop by today. And she said she'd arrange for other neighbors to do the same."

"I'm not leaving you," I repeated. "You stay with *me* when *I'm* sick."

"But you're my daughter."

"You're my mother."

Mom sighed. "Okay. You may stay home today."

"Thank you. What do you want for breakfast?"

My mother groaned. "Do I *have* to eat?"

"Only if you want to get well. You need strength. Plus, you make *me* eat when *I'm* sick."

Mom smiled. "You win. All right. Let me see. For breakfast I would like toast. And tea . . ." She trailed off.

I nodded. "Right. Toast, tea, hot cereal, fresh fruit."

"Oh, honey, I can't eat all that. Not this morning."

But I fixed it anyway. I served it to her on a tray, and she sat in her armchair and ate while I changed the sheets on her bed.

"You're a good nurse, Stacey," she told me.

"Thank you," I replied. "You still have to eat your breakfast." Mom was just picking around the edges of things.

"I really can't. I'll get sick."

I sighed. "Okay."

Mom climbed back into bed and lay against her pillows. "Nicely fluffed," she commented, and yawned. "Honestly, how could I be so tired? I slept all day yesterday and all last night and . . ." Mom's eyes drooped.

Before she could fall asleep I said, "Mom, I have to talk to you about something. It's important."

"*Really* important? Or can it wait a little while?"

"It's *pretty* important. Mom, what about this weekend?"

"This weekend?"

"You know, Dad's dinner. I'm supposed to go to New York."

"Right, the dinner. You can still go."

"And leave you?"

"Don't worry about me," said Mom firmly. "First of all, Friday is three days away. I'll be better by then. Second, I can arrange for Dee to look in on me. And she can run errands if I need anything."

"We-ell . . ."

"Stace, I'm falling asleep. We'll talk later. But plan on New York. It'll be fine. Trust me." Mom rolled over. The discussion had ended.

I tiptoed downstairs with her breakfast tray, ate my own breakfast, then cleaned up the kitchen. I kept picturing my mother lying on the gurney in the hospital emergency room, looking sicker than anyone should look, and saying, "I don't think this is the flu, Stacey."

How could I leave her? Maybe I should talk to my father, I thought. And then I realized he didn't even know Mom was sick. Nobody had called him. True, he and Mom weren't married anymore, but Dad had a right to know that his ex-wife had pneumonia. Especially if it meant I might have to miss our special weekend in New York.

I dialed the number of Dad's office. His secretary answered the phone.

"Hi," I said. "It's Stacey. Is my dad there?"

Dad has given his secretary instructions to put through all of my phone calls, no matter what. Even if he is in an important meeting. So a few minutes later I heard my father's voice say, "Hi, sweetie. What's wrong? Shouldn't you be in school? . . . Are you sick?"

"No, but Mom is," I answered. "Dad, she has pneumonia."

"Pneumonia! Is she in the hospital? Who are you staying with?"

"It's okay," I said. "She's at home. She went to the emergency room yesterday, but the doctor said she didn't need to stay." I told Dad that Mom hadn't been feeling well recently, and explained what had happened the day before.

"And you're sure she's all right now?" he said. "I mean, that she's as well as can be expected? She really shouldn't be in the hospital?"

"I'm positive. You can call Mrs. Pike, if you want to."

"Maybe I will." Dad sounded awfully concerned. Then he said, "Stacey, who's taking care of you?"

"Of me? I'm not sick. *I'm* taking care of *Mom.* But, Dad, I'm a little worried about this weekend, about coming to New York."

"I'll help you make arrangements for your mother," Dad assured me. "Maybe I can set up something with a visiting nurse service."

"Okay . . ."

"Brighten up," Dad went on. "Only three more days until Friday. Then you can take a break from school and sickness and everything else. Honey, I hope you know how important you are to me. To your mother *and* me. I will be honored to have you with me at the dinner. It will be a big moment and I can't think of anyone else I'd rather share it with."

I felt a knot form in my stomach. I just had to go to New York on Friday. I couldn't miss Dad's dinner, his big moment. But I couldn't leave Mom either. Why was I always choosing between my parents? There ought to be, I thought, a Divorce Handbook written just for kids to warn them about things like this. It would say, Even if you decide which parent to live with after the divorce, you will forever be choosing between them.

I wondered if this would go on when I was grown and married and had kids of my own. I could imagine Thanksgiving. I would say to my husband, "Dear, where will we spend Thanksgiving this year? At my mother's or my father's?" And my husband, whose parents would also be divorced, would reply, "Or at *my* mother's or *my* father's?"

At least when you are adults you could decide, "Let's spend Thanksgiving by ourselves this year." But then I would still worry about my parents who would have to spend the holiday alone.

Mabe I would write the Divorce Handbook

myself one day. I would ask all my friends whose parents are also divorced to be contributing writers and editors.

I decided not to worry about my decision for awhile. I was too busy caring for my mother. I had to see that she took her medicine, ate healthy food, and was never left alone in case she needed help getting to the bathroom or something.

Late that morning Mrs. Pike came over. "Stacey! I wasn't expecting to find you here. Why aren't you in school?"

Why wasn't I in school? For heaven's sake, my mother had pneumonia. Where did Mrs. Pike *think* I would be? "I'm taking care of Mom," I replied, surprised.

"She may be sick for awhile, hon."

This was a good point, and I had been giving it serious consideration. Mom probably *would* be sick for awhile. And I couldn't keep missing school. I miss enough of it when *I'm* sick. "I know," I said to Mrs. Pike, "but I'm taking care of everything. Leave it to me."

I had decided that if *I* couldn't be with my mother, then someone else should be. At all times. So I planned to contact Mom's friends and our neighbors and arrange for people to come stay with her while I was in school. They could come by in shifts. I would care for Mom the rest of the time. I would have to ask Mary Anne to find replacements for me for my sitting jobs during the next few days, but she would understand. She could call on our associate members, if she needed to.

While Mrs. Pike sat with my mother, I spread out a long piece of paper on the kitchen table. I drew up an hourly chart and marked off the times when I would be in school. Then I picked up the telephone.

"Hello, Mrs. Braddock?" I said. "This is Stacey McGill. Did you hear that my mom is sick? . . . Yeah, she has pneumonia. . . ."

When I hung up the phone I was able to fill in a couple of the boxes on the chart. By lunchtime, the entire chart had been filled in.

CHAPTER 7

I was proud of my chart. Not only did I fill it in, but the system actually worked. At seven-thirty on Wednesday morning as I was eating my breakfast and fixing Mom's at the same time, the doorbell rang. Mrs. Arnold had arrived. Mrs. Arnold, our neighbor, is the mother of Marilyn and Carolyn Arnold, twins for whom the members of the BSC often sit.

I ran to answer the door. "Thank you so much for coming!" I exclaimed.

"My pleasure," replied Mrs. Arnold.

"Now, my mom is still asleep," I told her. "At least, I think she is. She should wake up soon, though, and then please make her eat breakfast. She needs to keep her strength up. At eight-thirty she has to take one of these pills" (I held up a bottle) "and she can have aspirin if she wants it, since she's been getting headaches. She doesn't take another pill until ten, but you'll be off duty by then, and, let me see" (I checked my handy chart) "Mrs. Barrett will be here. I've left written instructions on the kitchen table for each person who will be taking care of Mom while I'm at school."

I noticed that Mrs. Arnold was smiling, and I raised my eyebrows.

"Oh, Stacey," she said, "it's just that this is such a switch: *my* coming to *your* house, and *your* giving *me* directions on how to care for someone."

I smiled, too, then. "Reverse baby-sitting," I agreed. "Mom-sitting."

Ten minutes later I was saying good-bye to my mother who was only about half-awake. "I'm sorry I have to leave," I told her, "but, well, I really can't miss too much school. Mrs. Arnold is here. She's down in the kitchen, but she'll come upstairs as soon as I leave. She's going to bring you your breakfast and later your pills, and she'll be here until nine-thirty. Then Mrs. Barrett is coming over, and after that, Mrs. Braddock and then Mrs. Prezzioso. I thought Mrs. Pike needed a break. Oh, and don't worry. Mrs. Prezzioso won't bring the baby with her. Andrea is going to stay at the Braddocks'. I'll come home right after school to relieve Mrs. P. Then you won't have another sitter until tomorrow when I leave for school again."

I tried to sound confident so Mom wouldn't worry. Then *I* ended up worrying all through school. Would my sitters show up when they were supposed to? What if someone forgot to come over? What if someone misplaced Mom's pills? What if, what if, what if? Several times I started toward the pay phones to call Mom between classes, but then I chickened out. What if she were sleeping and I woke her up?

As soon as school ended I dashed home. I ran through our front door and stopped to listen. The house was quiet.

Uh-oh.

"Mom? Mom!" I called.

Mrs. Prezzioso appeared at the top of the stairs. "Shh, Stacey," she whispered. "Your mother is sleeping."

"Did she eat her lunch?" I asked.

Mrs. P. was tiptoeing downstairs. "Mrs. Braddock gave it to her. I think she ate most of it. She's certainly been drinking fluids."

My mom was fine. Not fine as in all well, but fine as in the day had gone smoothly. The Mom-sitters had arrived on time, and my mother had been given her pills. I breathed a sigh of relief.

I spent the afternoon with my mother (once she had woken up). I decided she looked a little better than she had the day before, which meant she was making slow but steady progress.

At five-fifteen I was sitting in bed next to her, my shoes off, and we were watching a rerun of *The Dick Van Dyke Show*. Ordinarily, Mom would have been reading, but her head was aching. At any rate, my mother suddenly grabbed her wristwatch from the night table.

"Stacey!" she exclaimed. "You're supposed to be at a club meeting in fifteen minutes. You better find your shoes and get moving."

I shook my head. "I told Kristy I wouldn't be there today. Dawn is going to handle the treasury for me."

At that moment, Mom and I heard a door open and close downstairs. Then a voice called, "Hello?"

"That's Dee!" said Mom. Mrs. Pike had come over for a visit. "Now you can go to the meeting. Dee will stay with me. It's only for half an hour."

"We-ell . . ." I replied. Then I said to Mrs. Pike, "But who'll stay with your kids? Mallory's going to the meeting, too. Isn't she?"

"Mr. Pike is home early today, hon," she told me. "Now go on."

So I did. I hopped on my bike and rode to Claudia's.

Everyone was surprised to see me.

I enjoyed the meeting thoroughly. I was

glad to have a half hour in which to think about something other than school and Mom's health.

"Well," said Claudia after we had taken care of club business, "mail delivery sure has become an exciting event."

"It has?" I said.

"I'll say," agreed Mal. "The mail order stuff is starting to arrive."

"I was at the Braddocks' this afternoon," spoke up Jessi. "Matt got two patches. To sew on his clothes, I guess. One said BRACES ARE BEAUTIFUL. The other said OLD BOWLERS NEVER DIE; THEY END UP IN THE GUTTER. I have no idea why he wanted them. I don't think he has, either. But he sure liked getting mail."

"Yesterday," said Mal, "Vanessa received a bracelet-fastener and Nicky got a glass marble and a pamphlet about colleges in Minnesota."

"I hope Vanessa's bust-developer arrives soon," said Kristy, looking ruefully at her own chest, which is in need of development.

Mary Anne giggled. "Me, too."

Then Dawn said, "Not to change the subject, but did you decide what to do about this weekend, Stace?" (My friends knew about my dilemma. We usually know everything about each other.)

I shook my head. "I really don't want to

leave my mom, but you guys know how important the dinner is to my dad."

"Yeah," said Dawn, who has been caught between *her* parents a couple of times. (Maybe I would make Dawn the co-author of the Divorce Handbook. She's had as much divorce experience as I have.)

"I mean, everyone has been really helpful," I went on. I didn't want Mal to think I didn't appreciate her mother. "And I filled in the chart pretty quickly when I decided I had to go back to school. But I don't know. I'll feel guilty going off to New York for a weekend of fun, and leaving Mom behind fighting pneumonia. Even if she is going to be well cared for. I know she'd never do that if I were sick. She'd stay by my side."

"But," said Kristy, "she's the mother and you're the kid."

"So what? Mothers need to be taken care of, too. Anyway, if your mom was sick with pneumonia, would you, like, go to Disney World or something? That would look sort of selfish."

"Yeah, but you have a responsibility to your father," spoke up Jessi.

I closed my eyes briefly. "I know, I know."

"And it isn't like you can postpone your weekend with him. The dinner is on Friday and that's that."

"I *know*." I paused. Then I said. "Sorry, Jessi. I don't mean to sound crabby. But I've been having this very argument with myself since Monday night. I think, 'This is a once-in-a-lifetime honor for Dad. All he has asked is that I be with him for this important event.' Then I think, 'My mother has pneumonia. People can die from that.' The argument goes around and around. I know Mom isn't going to die. She's not sick enough. Still, it isn't like she has some little cold. Two days ago she was in the emergency room."

My friends shifted in their seats. Dawn was frowning fiercely. Kristy and Mal were gazing into space, asking the ceiling for answers. After a few moments, I said, "If you guys were in my shoes, what would you do?"

My friends voted. Three would go to New York, three would stay home.

"Some help you are," I said, but I was smiling.

After the meeting, I rode my bicycle home, and on the way, I finally made a decision. I could not abandon Mom. I would stay with her as much as I could until she was well again.

I knew Dad would not appreciate this news. I also knew I should give it to him as soon as possible. I phoned him after supper that evening.

"Dad," I said, "I have to tell you something. I have thought this over carefully. I'm not coming to New York this weekend. I'm going to stay here and take care of Mom."

"You're what?"

"I'm — I'm going to have to miss the dinner."

"But Stacey, this is important. Besides, you're my date for the evening."

"You could invite someone else," I suggested. "There's time."

"No," said Dad, sounding choked up. "That's not it. You're all I have. I don't know anyone else to invite. Just you. . . . You're all I have," he repeated.

"Maybe if you weren't a workaholic, there'd be something more in your life. But you're married to your job," I told my father.

Dad gasped, and I realized what I'd just said. I had practically accused him of being responsible for the divorce. I gasped, too. "Dad, I'm sorry," I cried. "I didn't mean to say that. Honest. But . . . but I can't leave Mom."

"I understand," said Dad quietly.

I wasn't sure he did.

CHAPTER 8

Thursday

I baby-sat for the Kuhn kids this afternoon, and the Great Mail Order Craze continues. Jake and Laurel absolutely could not wait for the mail to arrive today. Even Patsy was curious, although she's too little to order things yet, so nothing arrives for her. She likes examining the packages that come for her brother and sister, though. Yesterday Laurel even gave her one item — a sample of nail polish called Neon Nails because it's Day-Glo green. Patsy barely has nails, but she didn't care.

Anyway, the mail finally arrived and you should have seen the excitement among the kids in the neighborhood. The mailman must feel like a celebrity.

"Look! Look at me, Mary Anne!"

Laurel Kuhn greeted Mary Anne at the door in a state of great excitement. But Mary Anne couldn't see anything unusual about her. She looked at her from head to toe, feeling a little panicky. Clearly, Laurel felt she had made some great, obvious change. How could Mary Anne not notice it?

But before Mary Anne could think of an excuse, Laurel said, "My lipstick! It's my lipstick!" She was hopping around in excitement.

In all honesty, Mary Anne didn't see any lipstick on Laurel, even when she was actually looking for it. "Your lip — "

"It is *mood* lipstick," Laurel went on. "It came in the mail yesterday. It changes color. If you're angry, it is red. If you're happy, it is pink. If you're scared, it is yellow. If you're jealous, it is green."

"Boy. Pretty smart lipstick," said Mary Anne, who still could not detect *any* color on Laurel's lips.

Mary Anne entered the Kuhns' hallway then, and said hi to Jake, who's eight, and Patsy, who's five. (Laurel is six.) She and Mrs. Kuhn talked for several minutes before Mrs. Kuhn left to run errands. As soon as their mother was gone, the Kuhn kids pulled Mary

Anne into their rec room. "You have to see our stuff!" said Jake.

The couch in the rec room was covered with bottles and jars, pamphlets, cheap toys, and a few things Mary Anne couldn't identify. "What's this?" she asked, pointing to one of those unidentifiable objects.

"It's Poof," Jake informed her. "Stain remover."

" 'It can even remove ground-in dirt and grass stains,' " quoted Laurel.

"And what's this?" Mary Anne wanted to know. She pointed to a tiny vial.

"That," Jake said proudly, "is moondust."

"It really came from the moon," added Laurel. "Some astronauts brought a sack of it back with them."

"We are one of only twenty people in the whole world to own moondust," Jake went on. "We may be famous soon."

"That's *moon*dust?" Mary Anne said to Jake. "Are you sure?"

"The ad said."

"Oh."

"Guess how much it cost," demanded Laurel.

"Real moondust? Well, it must have been pretty expen — "

"Seventy-five cents," Laurel interrupted her.

"And I gave a quarter," spoke up Patsy. "We each did. So the moondust is part mine. I will be famous, too."

Ding-dong.

The Kuhn kids raced Mary Anne to the front door. Standing on the stoop were Buddy Barrett and Nicky Pike. Buddy was clutching a brown paper bag.

"The mail didn't come yet," announced Buddy, letting himself through the front door. (As an afterthought, he added, "Hi, everybody.")

"I know," replied Jake.

"Isn't the mail awfully late?" asked Mary Anne.

"Yup," spoke up Nicky, "but this is great because now we can wait for it. . . . Hi, everybody. . . . Gosh, I wonder where the mailman could *be*."

His truck is probably bogged down with free samples and jars of moondust, Mary Anne thought.

Patsy pointed to Buddy's paper bag. "What's in there?" she asked.

"It is very unbelievable," was Buddy's reply.

"Let's see!" squealed Laurel.

"Well, come outside," said Buddy. "I will show you while we wait for the mailman." Buddy settled himself on the Kuhns' stoop.

Nicky, Jake, Patsy, and Laurel crowded around him.

Buddy was just opening the bag when Mary Anne and the kids heard a shouted greeting. "Yo!" Haley Braddock was striding across the lawn, Matt at her side. Behind them trotted Vanessa and Margo Pike.

"Hi!" Mary Anne called.

And Patsy added, "Buddy is going to show us something!"

Buddy's audience had now doubled in size. He made a great show of unfolding the top of the bag and reaching inside. Then slowly, slowly he withdrew a tiny vial of . . . "Moondust," whispered Buddy. "This is actual dust from the actual moon. And an actual astronaut brought it back to Earth on an actual rocketship."

Jake's eyes had widened to nearly the size of tambourines. "Oh, my gosh. You're one of the twenty," he whispered. "I cannot believe it."

"What?" said Buddy, his brow furrowed.

"You — you're one of the twenty people who bought moondust. Did you read that little piece of paper that came with the jar?"

"Yeah."

"Laurel and Patsy and I bought moondust, too. We all chipped in. We are practically related to you then, Buddy."

70

"I guess you are also practically related to us Pikes," spoke up Margo. "I ordered some moondust, but it hasn't come yet."

Mary Anne noticed that Matt and Haley were signing to each other where they were perched at the bottom of the stoop. Presently Haley turned around and said to the rest of the kids, "Matt wants you to know that *he* is also your relative. He ordered moondust last week."

"This is so weird," said Jake in an eerie tone of voice. "Who would ever have guessed that most of the moondust owners would come from this very neighborhood?"

"You guys — " Mary Anne started to say.

"Hey, there's the mail truck!" shrieked Patsy.

"Where?" said Nicky.

"There."

The kids peered down the street. At a corner several blocks away, Mary Anne could just make out a blue shape that might be a mail truck.

"Let's go meet him!" cried Vanessa.

"All of you?" said Mary Anne. "No, don't swamp him. Why don't you wait until he's delivered the mail in this neighborhood. Then you can go from house to house and collect your stuff."

This idea seemed to appeal to the kids, although they had trouble waiting. They were not terribly patient. Nicky pulled Margo's ponytail. Patsy tickled Laurel's back and told her a spider was running down it. Buddy sang "I'm In Love With a Big Blue Frog" until the other kids couldn't take it any longer, and Patsy and Laurel put their hands over their ears.

The mail truck hadn't quite reached the Kuhns' when Buddy said, "Okay, can we go to *my* house now? The mail must be there."

"All right," agreed Mary Anne.

The kids, all nine of them, took off running.

"Wait for me!" called Mary Anne.

Buddy, slightly ahead of the pack of kids, reached his mailbox at the same time as his sister Suzi, who had zoomed across the Barretts' lawn. They nearly crashed into each other, then grabbed for the catch on the box at the same time. They struggled briefly.

"I want to open it!" said Buddy.

"No, me!" exclaimed Suzi.

Mary Anne put her hands over the kids'. "Open it together," she said.

They did. Then they scrambled to grab the loot inside while the other kids watched enviously.

"It's here!" cried Buddy.

"It came!" cried Suzi.

"What's here? What came?" asked Mary Anne.

"My stamp-licker," said Buddy. (Mary Anne wondered what was wrong with sponges. Or for that matter, with tongues.)

"My moondust," said Suzi.

Silence fell over the group. At last Haley repeated, "Your moondust?"

"Yes!" Suzi was ripping into a small mailing envelope, oblivious to the stunned reaction of her brother and friends. She held up the familiar vial. "Here it is! Real dust from the moon! I wonder what this says." She held a folded piece of white paper toward Buddy. He took it, but didn't look at it.

"I know what it says," Buddy told her dispiritedly. "It says a lie."

"Huh?" Suzy was gazing at her moondust.

Buddy glanced at Mary Anne, then at his friends. Haley shook her head slightly. Buddy considered for a moment. Finally he said, "Never mind. It just tells about moondust, Suzi. That was a cool thing to order."

"Thanks."

"So, Buddy. Did you get anything else?" asked Mary Anne brightly.

Buddy looked through the mail again. "Just the stamp-licker, I guess. Come on, you guys. Let's see what you got."

The kids left Suzi and her moondust on the Barretts' lawn. They ran down the sidewalk toward the Pikes' house. Mary Anne wasn't sure, but she had a feeling the kids were moving somewhat more slowly.

In the Pikes' mailbox, Nicky found a mustache comb.

In the Braddocks' mailbox, Haley found a trial-size tube of ointment guaranteed to erase crow's feet in seven to ten days.

In the Kuhns' mailbox, Jake found a pamphlet titled, "So You're Going to Cater a Wedding."

The kids examined their treasures.

"This stamp-licker doesn't work," complained Buddy.

"I don't *have* crow's feet around my eyes," said Haley. "What am I supposed to do with this ointment?"

"And what are *you* going to do with a mustache comb?" Vanessa asked Nicky.

"I could give it to Dad."

"He doesn't have a mustache, either."

"Oh, yeah."

Jake threw away his wedding pamphlet. "Now what?" he asked his friends. "What do you guys want to do now?"

"Order more stuff?" suggested Buddy.

But they couldn't. The kids were completely broke.

CHAPTER 9

While Mary Anne was chasing the neighborhood kids from mailbox to mailbox, I was at home with my mother.

I was watching her nap. She was not sleeping peacefully. She kept coughing.

"She had a bad morning," Mrs. Braddock had reported when I came home from school. "And her temperature is up a bit."

"Do you think she needs to go back to the hospital?" I asked, alarmed.

Mrs. Braddock didn't seem worried. "No, I think she just needs to sleep. This happens sometimes. She'll probably feel better tomorrow."

"I hope so," I said. Immediately, I began reconsidering a decision I had just made. The decision was not to decide. I mean, decide between my parents. It had occurred to me that I could take care of both of them. I could leave for New York on Friday afternoon as I had planned, go to the dinner with my father, then come back to Stoneybrook first thing Saturday morning. I would be away from Mom for less than twenty-four hours *and* I wouldn't disappoint my father. I was still nervous about leaving Mom overnight, but I could line up people to stay with her then just like I did while I was at school.

Now, watching her sleep and remembering what Mrs. Braddock had said about her bad morning, I wondered if I really could leave her on Friday night. Then I replayed the horrible phone conversation with my father.

I sighed.

And Mom woke up.

She rolled over and saw me sitting in the chair by her bed. "Hi, sweetie," she mumbled. She reached for the box of tissues.

"Hi. How are you feeling?"

"Better, I think."

"Really?"

"Yeah. I'm actually chilly. I was burning up before, so I threw off the covers." Mom pulled them over her again.

"Let's take your temperature," I suggested. I found the thermometer and shook it down. "Normal!" I was able to announce a few minutes later. "Maybe Mrs. Braddock was right. You just needed to sleep."

"You know what? I think I'm actually hungry," said my mother.

"Hey, great! I'll fix you a snack."

Mom ate the snack and then said she thought she might like a cup of tea, so I fixed that, too. And then Mrs. Pike dropped by. While they drank tea together in the bedroom, I called my father.

My hands shook as I dialed the number of his office.

"Hi," I said to his secretary. "It's Stacey. Is my dad there?"

"Hold on a minute."

When my father got on the line he sounded hesitant. "Stace?"

"Hi, Dad. Um, listen, I've been thinking. How about if I go to the dinner — "

"Fantastic!" exclaimed Dad.

" — but I come back to Stoneybrook early Saturday morning. I won't stay for the weekend, but I won't miss the dinner, either."

"That sounds fair."

"I still have to figure out what to do about Mom while I'm gone."

"She really can't stay by herself?"

"I don't think she should."

Then Dad and I both spoke at the same time.

"I'll call a visiting nurse service," he said.

"I'll talk to our neighbors," I said.

Click, click.

"Oh, Dad, hold on. We're getting another call." I pressed the call waiting button. "Hello?" (I just love call waiting.)

"Hello, this is Dr. Becker's office. I'm calling about Mrs. McGill's blood tests."

"Oh, yes!" I said. "This is her daughter. Hold on. I'll get right back to you." I pressed the button again. "Dad? I have to go. That's the doctor with Mom's tests."

Dad hung up and I talked to the doctor. Then Mom talked to her.

"It's pneumonia," said Mom when she got off the phone, "and only pneumonia. All the other tests were negative." She smiled at Mrs. Pike.

"All what other tests?" I wanted to know.

"Oh, the doctors wanted to be positive about the pneumonia diagnosis. They wanted to be able to rule out a few other possibilities."

Boy. I was glad I hadn't known about *that*. I would have spent the last three days worrying that the doctors had misdiagnosed Mom and she really did have leukemia or something.

Mrs. Pike had to leave then. I wanted to talk to her about Friday night. Uh-oh — I hadn't told *Mom* about Friday night.

"Mom?" I said. She was repositioning herself in bed. "I just talked to Dad. This is what

I finally decided about the weekend. I'll go to New York tomorrow after school and come back first thing Saturday morning. How does that sound?"

"Perfect."

"You're sure?"

"Positive."

"Okay. I'm going to talk to Mrs. Pike. I'll make sure someone is here with you at all times." I paused. "Wow, I have a lot to do. I have to pack — I can't forget my new outfit. I have to talk to the neighbors. Let's see. I better tell Kristy I won't be at the meeting tomorrow. Dawn will have to be the treasurer. Oh, and I have to find the train schedule."

As you can imagine, the rest of the afternoon was fairly hectic. I remembered that I also needed to catch up on some homework, and of course I had to take care of Mom.

First things first. I sat at the desk in my room, my math book opened, a fresh sheet of paper in front of me.

I could not concentrate.

So I turned on my radio, set my suitcase on the bed, and began to pack. In went the new outfit, in went my nightgown, in —

"Stace?" called Mom.

"Yeah?" I dashed into her room.

"Sorry to bother you, honey, but I need another box of Kleenex."

I got her the Kleenex. Then I returned to my packing.

In went my underwear.

"Stacey?"

"Yeah?"

"I'm *really* sorry — "

"Don't worry about it. That's what I'm here for."

" — but I've lost the remote control for the TV."

I retrieved the remote control from between the bed and the dresser.

I went back to my room. And it occurred to me that I should take care of BSC business before I did anything else. So I phoned Dawn.

"Hi, it's me," I said. "Listen, I can't go to the meeting tomorrow — "

"You mean you decided to go to New York?" cried Dawn.

"Just overnight. Just for the dinner."

"That's a good solution."

"Yeah, if I can find overnight Mom-sitters. And I have to pack, of course. Oh, and miss tomorrow's meeting. Which is why I'm calling. Can you get ready to be treasurer for the day?"

"Sure. No problem. It won't even be a dues day."

"No. Just remember to give Kristy money to pay Charlie. We owe him. And someone might need money to replace stuff in a Kid-Kit. I think that'll be all."

"Cool. See you in school tomorrow."

"Okay. . . . Dawn?"

"Yeah?"

"Do you ever resent your parents for getting divorced?"

"Lots of times. Why?"

"I don't know. I guess just because if Mom and Dad were still together, I wouldn't be in such a mess right now. I mean about the weekend. If we all lived in New York, then Mom would have been Dad's date for the dinner, and when she got sick, well, I'm not sure what would have happened, but somehow I don't think I would have been affected. Not *so* affected, anyway. Not caught in the middle."

"I don't think I get caught in the middle as often as you," said Dawn thoughtfully. "But when I do, it's an even bigger problem because I feel pulled from coast to coast. My decisions involve plane trips and time changes and stuff."

"Which would you rather have?" I asked Dawn. "All the fighting before the divorce, or all the problems after the divorce?"

"Neither."

I giggled. "That isn't a choice."

"Oh. Then I choose the right to remain silent."

"Daw-*awn!*"

"Also, to be completely fair to parents, I would like to point out that not every divorce creates problems. Some work out pretty well." Dawn paused. "But if a genie ever floated out of a bottle and said I could have one wish? I'd wish that Mom and Dad were still *happily* married."

"Me, too. Oh, well. I better call Kristy now. Thanks for being treasurer tomorrow. I'll see you in school, Dawn."

CHAPTER 10

After Dawn and I got off the phone, I called Kristy as I had planned. Of course, she was understanding about the meeting. Then I sat down to my homework again. I worked diligently for fifteen or twenty minutes, but I had to stop when I felt (and heard) my stomach growling. Dinnertime. I needed to eat, and hoped Mom would want to eat again, too. So I abandoned my homework for the second time that day.

I poked my head into Mom's room. She was watching one of those ancient sitcoms on a cable station that shows nothing but ancient sitcoms. It was called *Our Miss Brooks*. She looked pretty contented.

"Mom? Do you want some dinner?"

"Dinner? I feel as if I just ate."

"You did," I said, laughing, "but you should eat again. It would be good for you.

You don't have to eat a lot. How about some soup?"

"Okay," replied Mom. "Thanks, honey."

I fixed Mom a bowl of vegetable soup, plus crackers and peanut butter. Peanut butter is full of protein. Also calories.

I fixed myself a frozen dinner. While it was in the oven, I made phone calls. I needed to line up Mom-sitters. This evening was my only chance to do it. I'd be leaving for New York right after school the next day. I searched around for the Mom-sitter chart, but I couldn't find it. I'd thought it was on my desk with the mess that was homework, but it must have become part of some other mess. I hadn't realized how much time my mother probably devoted to tidying up the house each day. I thought I was a relatively neat person, but now that I took a good look around, I realized that . . . well, that the sink was piled high with dirty dishes, the laundry basket was overflowing, and the house was a visual history of everything that had gone on in it since Monday. My school things were flung around the foyer. A trail of mail led from the living room upstairs to Mom's bedroom. Empty soup cans and cereal boxes littered the kitchen. How did Mom keep up with the house *and* do her temp work *and* look for a full-time job? No wonder she had pneumonia.

I gave up looking for the list and just started phoning people. I had called Mrs. Kishi, Mrs. Barrett, and Mrs. Prezzioso when I realized my frozen dinner was more than done. I'd forgotten to set the timer.

I sniffed the air. Whew! "Mrs Prezzioso," I said, "I have to go! I have to turn off the oven. . . . What? . . . Sure, you can call back later. I still need people to fill in from midnight until eight A.M."

When I got off the phone I made a dash for the oven, and hauled that dinner out of there. It wasn't exactly charred, but it certainly wasn't tender. Oh, well. It was edible.

I wolfed down the dinner and was trying to decide whether to attempt my homework again or whether to telephone Mrs. Braddock about Mom-sitting when our bell rang. Then Mal's mom opened the back door.

"Hello?" she called.

"Hi, Mrs. Pike!" I replied. "Come on in."

Mrs. Pike looked around the kitchen. She wrinkled her nose.

"I know! Don't say anything," I exclaimed. "I burned my dinner. And the kitchen was already a mess. I haven't done a bit of house-work, I'm behind on my homework, and now I'm going to New York tomorrow for the night and I'm not sure who's staying with Mom and I haven't even finished packing. Plus — "

"Stacey! Relax," said Mrs. Pike. "You need a break. I have a suggestion. How about if you finish packing while I line up help for your mom. After that, why don't you do your homework over at our house. That would be a change of scenery, and the kids would love to see you."

"Well . . ."

"Go on, honey. I'm happy to stay with your mother for awhile."

So I caved in. I ran to my room and finished packing. I told Mom I was going to be at the Pikes' for not more than two hours. Then I gathered up my books and dashed through the yards to Mal's.

Vanessa let me in the back door. "Hi! You came!" she cried. "Mom said you might. I'm glad you did." She paused. "I know you have to do your homework," she went on, eyeing my books, "because you are here as a guest, not as our baby-sitter. So go on upstairs. I'll try to keep the little kids from bothering you."

"Thanks, Vanessa," I said. I headed for Mallory and Vanessa's bedroom. Halfway there, I met Mal coming downstairs.

"Hi," she greeted me. "Are you here to work?" (I nodded.) "Well, the upstairs is too noisy. Let's go to the rec room."

Mal and I tried to arrange the rec room like a study hall at school. That took nearly twenty minutes. As soon as we were finished, and had prudently seated ourselves back to back so we couldn't be distracted by looking at each other, Margo bounced into the room.

"This is a study hall," Mal informed her sister.

"A what?"

"A study hall. We are working very hard here. We cannot be disturbed."

"You already are disturbed," said Adam, following his sister into the room.

"Very funny," replied Mal.

Adam grinned. "I thought so."

"Well, anyway, we *are* trying to study."

"But I just want to show Stacey one thing," said Margo.

Mal sighed. "What is it?"

"My necktie-knotter. It came in the mail today."

I raised my eyebrows. "Oh . . . awesome. I guess you're going to give it to your dad? Or to one of your brothers?"

"Hey," said Adam, "Margo, I'll trade you the neckie-knotter for my slice 'n' dice. How's that? I could use a necktie-knotter."

Margo considered the offer. "What does the slice 'n' dice do?"

Adam snorted. "It slices and dices."

"It slices and dices *what*?"

"Oh, vegetables, eggs, meat, almost anything. You could make an entire salad in two and a half minutes."

"All right. Let's trade."

"Good. Hand over the necktie-knotter."

Margo and Adam exchanged gadgets. They left us alone to work.

I attacked a math problem. If $x = 3.2$, then $3x$ —

"Guys? Guys?" Claire was hesitating at the entrance to our study hall.

"We're working," Mal told her. "Whatever it is, go ask Daddy."

"I can't. I want to show Stacey something."

Mal looked at me sympathetically. "They haven't seen you in awhile," she explained. "Sorry about this."

"That's okay. I don't really mind."

Claire had been looking hopefully at us. Now she smiled. She produced something from behind her back and handed it to me. "This is Vanessa's bust-developer thing," she whispered.

"Why are *you* showing it to me?" I whispered back.

"Because Vanessa is too embarrassed. I'm not sure why."

Mallory giggled. She tried to hide her giggle, but she wasn't successful.

Claire eyed her. "What *is* this thing?" she asked.

"Um," said Mal and I.

"Well, what's a bust?"

"Um."

"Well?" said Claire.

"Go ask Daddy," suggested Mal.

"I already did. He said to ask Mommy, but she isn't here."

Mal tried to change the subject. "Does Vanessa know you have her bust-developer?"

Claire shrugged. "Maybe."

"I think you ought to return it to her."

"Okay, I will. As soon as you tell me what it is."

At that moment, Vanessa stomped into the room. "There it is!" she declared. She snatched the bust-developer from Claire, stuffed it under her shirt, and ran upstairs.

Claire followed her, calling, "But what is it? What is it?"

Mal and I grinned at each other. We hadn't even tried to resume our studying when we heard a frustrated cry from the kitchen. It was Margo bellowing, "This thing doesn't slice *or* dice! You gypped me, Adam!"

"I did not!" Adam's voice came from some other part of the house. "*You* gypped *me*! This necktie-knotter makes knots all right, but they aren't necktie knots. They're just knots you can't undo!"

Before Mal and I knew what had hit us, we

were surrounded by kids and gadgets —
Margo with the slice 'n' dice, Adam with the
necktie-knotter, Claire and Vanessa struggling
over the bust-developer, and Nicky, Byron,
and Jordan standing around watching.

"Mal put her hand over her ears. "WE ARE
TRYING TO WORK!" she bellowed. "Take
these things to Dad!"

Silence fell. Several moment passed. Then
Jordan said, as if he hadn't heard Mal at all,
"I ordered four things through the mail. Two
of them don't work. The other two work, but
I don't need them."

"The necktie-knotter doesn't work," commented Adam.

"The slice 'n' dice doesn't work," said
Margo.

"Vanessa? Does the bust-developer work?"
asked Claire.

"I DON'T KNOW!"

"You know what I really wish I had?" said
Jordan. "A yo-yo. Everyone in my class has
one."

"Same here," said Adam and Byron.

"In my class, too," agreed Vanessa.

Nicky nodded. "Yo-yos are cool. They come
in fluorescent colors. David Michael Thomas
even has one that lights up."

"Maybe you can find an offer for mail-order
yo-yos," said Mal.

Byron was shaking his head. "I haven't seen any. But even if I had, it wouldn't matter. I don't have any money left for a yo-yo. I'm all out."

Mal's other brothers and sisters agreed. They had spent their money on bust-developers and necktie-knotters. They were broke. Mal made one final suggestion: "Maybe Dad will give you advances on your allowances," she said.

At that, the kids flew from the room and stampeded upstairs.

Mallory and I returned to our work. When I left for home later that evening, my assignments were not exactly finished, but I was in a much better frame of mind. I kept imagining Claire chasing after Vanessa and the bust-developer, crying, "But what is it? What is it?" And I did feel bad that the Pike kids were out of money, but they *had* brought it on themselves, and the situation *was* sort of funny.

When I went to bed that night, I actually — for the first time since Monday — relaxed and fell into a deep sleep.

CHAPTER 11

"Stacey! Hey, Stacey!"

I was standing on the steps at the front entrance to Stoneybrook Middle School. Kids streamed around me, shouting and calling to one another, eager to leave school and start their weekends. I was looking for Mrs. Pike, who was going to drive me to the train station, so I wasn't expecting to hear a male voice calling my name.

"Stacey!" the voice called again.

I became aware of frantic movement somewhere to my left. I turned my head — and there was Sam, waving to me from across the lawn.

"Hi!" I called back excitedly. Sam had never stopped by my school before. I think he was embarrasseu to be seen at SMS, since he is a mighty high school student. I trotted over to him.

"Walk you home?" asked Sam.

"I wish you could, but I'm not going home," I had to reply.

Darn, darn, darn. Or as Karen Brewer would say, boo. Double boo. This was the one day I couldn't go with Sam, because of stupid old New York.

"Oh." Sam looked crestfallen.

"I'm going to New York to see my dad," I explained.

"I thought your mom was sick."

"She is, but . . . oh, never mind. It's too hard to explain. I'll be back tomorrow," I added hopefully.

But all Sam said was, "Well, have fun. See you around."

Darn, *darn*, DARN.

"Stacey!"

This time I recognized Mrs. Pike's voice. She was calling to me from the parking lot. I waved sadly to Sam, then ran to the Pikes' car, where I nearly crashed into Mal and Jessi who were running from another direction. They were coming along for the ride to the station. Mrs. Pike leaned over and opened the front door for me.

"Thank you for picking me up," I said breathlessly as Mal and Jessi climbed into the backseat with Claire. "Is my suitcase here?"

"I have it!" said Claire proudly. It was sitting in her lap. My suitcase was actually just an overnight bag. Basically all I had ended up packing was my new outfit, a nightgown, and clean underwear. I was traveling light. I planned to wear the same outfit tomorrow that I was wearing now.

"Thanks, Claire," I replied. I turned to Mrs. Pike. "How's Mom?"

"Just fine, honey. Nothing to worry about. Mrs. Arnold is with her, and she plans to stay until dinnertime. Then Mrs. Braddock will take over."

"Okay."

At the station, everyone piled out of the car. Mal, Jessi, and Claire pretended they were seeing me off on a long trip.

"Don't forget to write!" called Jessi.

"I'll think of you every day!" called Mal.

"Have fun in Spain!" called Claire.

Mrs. Pike rolled her eyes.

The ride to New York was long enough to allow me to finish my math homework and start an English assignment. I was halfway into the English assignment when I realized the train wasn't moving. I looked at my watch. Uh-oh.

I don't know what caused the train delay, but we rolled into Grand Central Station in New York City a full half an hour late.

"Stacey!" exclaimed Dad when we found

each other at the information booth. "I thought you'd never get here."

I groaned. "Me, too. We just sat on the tracks — right outside Grand Central — for *half* an *hour*."

Dad gave me a bear hug. Then he said, "We better get a move-on." (I have never known just what a "move-on" is.) "We're cutting this close."

My father and I hurried out of the station and caught a cab on 42nd Street. Unfortunately, it was now rush hour, so the ride to Dad's apartment that should have taken about twelve minutes took nearly forty-five. I know Dad wanted to grumble to our cab driver, but he didn't, because the driver had posted this really defensive sign on the back of his seat, right in front of Dad's knees. It read:

Please be aware that:
— I know where I am going.
— I know how to drive.
— I have a complete grasp of the English language.

I pointed to the sign and giggled, which made Dad smile, but didn't get us to his apartment any faster.

When we did get there, we raced inside and

I hurried to my bedroom. (Well, Dad and I call it my bedroom, but somehow it doesn't feel like mine. I don't stay in it often enough. It feels like a motel room.)

"What time does the dinner start?" I called to Dad.

"We're supposed to be there at six-thirty."

"Six-thirty? Yikes!" I yelped as I opened my overnight bag.

"I know. We're running late. We didn't allow time for delays."

I paused. "Um, did we allow time for ironing?"

"What?" said Dad, poking his head into my room.

"Well, it's just that I had to do my packing yesterday, and now my outfit is sort of smushed. I need to iron it. Badly."

Dad sighed. He did not say a word, but he set up the ironing board and plugged in the iron for me.

I think the extra delay was worth it. When I finally emerged from my room, wearing the new, ironed outfit (with tasteful Dad-type jewelry), my hair combed and shining, my father just stared at me. After a few moments, he managed to say, "You look . . . like your mother." Then he added hurriedly, "You look beautiful, sweetie. Absolutely perfect."

"Thanks," I whispered. Then, hating to

break the spell, I said, "Um, it's already six-twenty-five, Dad."

We caught another cab. This one rushed us to a very fancy hotel on Madison Avenue. And I mean, it *rushed* us. We squealed around corners, jerked to stops, then jerked into motion again. I have never made such good use of that strap that hangs by the window as I did that evening. When we screeched to a halt in front of the hotel, I said, "Dad? Do I still have all my teeth? I think I can hear them rattling around in my head."

The cabbie shot me a dirty look in the rear-view mirror then, but he didn't say anything because Dad was in the middle of trying to figure out how much to tip him.

We stepped out of the taxi, and Dad took my arm and led me into the hotel. We followed the signs to the MCGILL PARTY.

"They made *signs* for this?" I whispered to Dad.

He just smiled at me.

When we reached the MCGILL PARTY, I glanced at a clock on the wall. Six-forty-three. Not too bad.

We walked through a pair of plain wooden double doors and into . . . a ballroom. I was awed. Crystal chandeliers hung from the ceiling. The floor was carpeted in gold — except for a large bare area in the center of the room.

(I would have to ask Dad about that later.) The tables were covered with white cloths. At every place setting was gleaming silverware and a crystal bud vase holding a single red rose; in the middle of each table was a large arrangement of red and yellow roses.

"Whoa. All this for you, Dad?" I whispered.

He didn't answer the question, but simply replied, "I'm so glad you're here to share the evening with me."

So was I. When Dad had talked about a fancy dinner, I never imagined he meant *this* fancy . . . or important. My father must mean an awful lot to his company.

I was gazing at those chandeliers again when I realized Dad was talking to some people. "Stacey?" he said, and I dragged my eyes away from the glitter of the crystal. "I want you to meet Mr. Davis, the president." The *president*? I thought wildly. . . . Oh, the president of the *com*pany. "And this is Mrs. Barnes, the executive vice-president."

"It's nice to meet you, Stacey," said Mr. Davis.

"You must be very proud of your father," said Mrs. Barnes.

"Oh, I am." I was absolutely awestruck.

"Well, we better get this affair underway," added Mr. Davis.

Dad took my elbow. "Time to sit down," he said.

"Which table is ours?" I asked.

"I'll show you." Dad led me through the fifteen or so small round tables to a long banquet table where a podium was set up. "We're at the head table," he said, "with Mr. Davis and Mrs. Barnes and the other executives."

"Whoa," was the only word I managed to utter.

We slid along between the banquet table and the wall, reading the placecards, until we reached the podium. Dad's place was next to the podium; mine was next to his. We sat down. I felt breathless. Stoneybrook seemed a million miles away.

Here is what we did at the dinner that evening: ate and listened to speeches.

The dinner itself was very fancy. Lots of courses. First came a beautiful . . . well, I'm not sure what you would call two jumbo shrimps on a piece of lettuce. An hors d'oeuvre, maybe? Then came a tiny bowl of consommé.

Then came a speech. Mrs. Barnes gave a sort of pep talk to the company.

After that, someone who seemed to be a good friend of my father presented a slide show. It was about Dad and his years with the company. A lot of the pictures made the dinner guests hoot and clap and laugh. *I* was even in one picture. The photo showed Dad sitting at his desk at work, holding me on his lap. I was, like, five years old, and wearing a truly hideous dress, falling-down socks, and ratty sneakers. But the laughter that followed was friendly, so I didn't mind too much.

When the slide show was over, the waiters served sherbet. I couldn't eat mine, of course, but I was still curious about it. "Why are they serving dessert?" I asked Dad. "They haven't served dinner yet." Or had they? Maybe those two shrimps were dinner.

"This is to clear your palate," Dad whispered. "Dinner is next."

Whew. While everyone else was eating the sherbet, I excused myself and went to the lobby. I had noticed a bank of pay phones there, and I wanted to call Mom and check on her.

Mrs. Braddock answered the call and said Mom was fine but that she was sleeping. I returned to the dinner.

I reached my place just in time to be served a plate of roast beef and vegetables — and to hear another speech.

Then came the salad course. *After* dinner? Oh, well. I decided I had been away from New

York too long. I was losing my grip on sophistication.

I ate the salad, called Mom again (she was still fine and still asleep), and this time returned just as coffee was being poured and dessert was being served. Dessert was white chocolate mousse, but guess what the waiter brought *me*: a goblet of fresh fruit, topped with a strawberry.

Then came another speech. This one was made by . . . my father. He didn't seem at all nervous as he adjusted the microphone, or as he talked about how important the company was to him. He spoke for nearly ten minutes. The very last thing he said was, "I am especially honored that tonight my daughter Stacey could be here to share in this event. Thank you all very much. And thank you, Stacey."

Dad started to sit down then, but Mr. Davis stopped him. He joined my father at the podium and said, "Not so fast," which made everyone hoot and laugh again. Mrs. Barnes stood up, too, and together she and Mr. Davis presented Dad with a plaque, thanked him for his years of service, and congratulated him on his new position.

That was the end of the speeches. Also the food. I checked the time. Ten o'clock! Oh, my lord. I wanted to catch the six-thirty A.M. train. Luckily, people were starting to get up then.

"Okay, Dad, we better leave, too," I said.

"Now? Before we have a chance to dance?"

The people who had stood up were now moving around the square of bare floor. (So *that's* what it was for.)

"I have to get up at four-thirty tomorrow morning," I informed Dad.

"You're kidding."

I shook my head.

Reluctantly, Dad left his party.

CHAPTER 12

I am not at my best early in the morning. I am particularly not at my best at four-thirty in the morning.

Neither is my father.

Guess what time we had gone to bed the night before. Midnight. We were running on a measly four and a half hours of sleep.

See, Dad couldn't just walk away from his dinner. He (and I) had to say good night to Mr. Davis and Mrs. Barnes and about fifteen other people. Then, as we walked through the ballroom to those double doors, people kept stopping Dad to talk to him. So between that and a ride with New York's slowest cab driver, we didn't turn out the lights in the apartment until 11:54.

When the alarm rang at four-thirty, I truly could not believe it. "Didn't I just go to bed?" I mumbled into the darkness.

I stumbled to the bathroom and washed my

face in an attempt to wake up, but I hadn't bothered to turn on a light, so the water didn't do me much good.

"Dad?" I called. I knocked on his door, then returned to my room, sat on my bed, and rubbed my eyes. At last I dared to turn on a light.

"Oh, spare me," I moaned, squinting into the brightness.

Finally I dredged up enough energy to take a shower. When I finished, Dad took one. I got dressed (in yesterday's school clothes) and started Mr. Coffee for Dad.

"Do we have anything for breakfast?" I called from the kitchen.

"Bagels," Dad replied. "In the bread drawer."

Oh, goody. Real New York bagels. I set them on the table along with cream cheese and orange juice.

Soon my father stumbled out of his room and directly to Mr. Coffee. He poured himself a cup, and then we sat silently at the table.

Dad blinked, trying to focus his eyes. After a moment he said, "What happened last night, Stacey?"

I swallowed a large mouthful of bagel. "Huh?"

"All of a sudden you wanted to leave."

"I was hoping to get to bed early. I was

trying to prevent us from feeling exactly the way we feel now."

"I had no idea you would intend to get up at four-thirty in the morning."

"I told you I wanted to take an early train."

"I know, but I didn't realize that would involve walking out before the dinner was over."

"If that bothered you, how come you didn't say so last night?"

"I didn't want to spoil the evening. But I swan, Stacey." (He swanned?) "You kept getting up and leaving the room during the ceremony, and then for us to be the very first people to leave, well . . ."

"Look," I said, bristling, "at least I *came*, didn't I? I was trying to do what I thought was best. I was trying to be there for you *and* Mom."

Dad just nodded his head.

We barely said two words to each other between then and the time Dad escorted me to my train at Grand Central. At ten after six, when we entered the station through the row of swinging doors off of Vanderbilt, Grand Central was a busy place, but a quietly busy place compared to the bustle of commotion which it would become in a couple of hours. A few stores had opened — mostly donut and coffee stands — and the newsstand was in full swing. Short lines of people stood at the ticket windows, waiting drowsily. Along one wall, about twelve men were sleeping. They huddled in cardboard boxes or in piles of rags, clutching their possessions, even while they slept.

Dad saw me looking at them. "Sometimes now they kick them out of the station at night," he said. "They tell them they have to sleep somewhere else."

Those were the first complete sentences Dad had uttered since breakfast. He was trying to make up with me. He and Mom used to have this rule that they couldn't go to bed mad at each other. If they were angry they would have to talk out their problem before they could go to sleep. (I guess this policy hadn't worked too well.) Anyway, I knew that now Dad didn't want me to leave for Stoneybrook while we were angry. I didn't want to do that, either.

So I said, "They kick out the homeless? But then where do they go?"

Dad shrugged. "The streets. Doorways. Subways. But sometimes they get kicked out of the subways, too."

"Remember Judy?" I asked.

"Judy?"

"The homeless woman who lived in our old neighborhood. Before the divorce."

"Oh, *Judy*. Of course."

"I wonder whatever happened to her."

"Don't know."

"And I wonder what happens to homeless people when they die. They must die right in the streets. Or in a park. Or even here in Grand Central. But you never hear about that. You never hear on the news that someone found a dead person in the train station."

"Stacey!" exclaimed Dad.

"Well, you don't." I paused. "You know, there's an awful lot to worry about."

"But that isn't your job," countered my father.

We were approaching the gate to my train. A ragged man, his feet wrapped in newspapers, was standing at the gate, his hand extended toward us.

"Wait, Dad," I said. I opened my purse (not a good thing to do in the streets or train stations of NYC, but sometimes you don't have much choice), and found a five-dollar bill. I gave it to the man.

"Thank you," he whispered. "God bless you."

"You're welcome. . . . Um, good luck."

"Stacey, that was very nice of you," Dad said gently after we had passed the man, "but you can't take care of everybody, you know."

I nodded. "But I can try."

I found a seat on the train. Dad waited on the platform until the doors closed. We waved to each other through a window. Then as the train eased down the track, my father turned and walked off.

I slept all the way home.

Mrs. Pike met my train in Stoneybrook. "Hi," she said stiffly as I slid into the front seat and closed the door. She pulled out of the parking lot before I had even buckled my seat belt.

"Is anything wrong?" I asked nervously. Maybe Mrs. Pike resented spending so much time helping Mom and me.

"There's a slight problem at your house," she admitted.

I must have turned pale or looked like I was going to faint, because Mrs. Pike added in a rush, "Oh, it isn't your mother! She's just fine. It's a matter of scheduling. You'll see when we get there."

I had a feeling I was in Big Trouble.

Mrs. Pike parked in our driveway, and I dashed into the house ahead of her. I heard voices coming from the kitchen. Was Mom out of bed?

No. In the kitchen were Mrs. Kishi, Mrs. Arnold, and a woman in a white uniform. They were drinking coffee.

"Hi," I said uncertainly. "Where's my mother?"

"She's upstairs, asleep," answered Mrs. Arnold.

Mrs. Pike joined us in the kitchen then. "Stacey," she said, "this is Miss Koppelman. She's from a visiting nurse service in Stamford. Your father hired her to stay with your mother last night."

"He did? He didn't tell me. At least, I don't think he told me."

"And Mrs. Kishi has been here since midnight," Mallory's mother went on. "She thought she was supposed to be here until eight this morning, and Mrs. Arnold arrived at six."

"Oh, no. I'm so sorry."

Mrs. Kishi smiled. "Don't worry," she said. "It isn't your fault."

I never did find out just who had lined up who. Mrs. Pike and I had both been phoning neighbors on Thursday afternoon and evening — without checking with each other. We told people to call us back, or that we'd call them back, and I didn't keep track of anything. My scheduling system had failed.

Mary Anne's mom had also arrived at midnight on Friday, but had gone home. Plus, after the nurse and neighbors left on Saturday morning, there was peace until ten A.M., when two other neighbors arrived. I was more confused than they were. (But I think Miss Koppelman had been the most confused of all.)

I apologized to the two neighbors who had shown up, and told them they could go home. Then I told my mom she was in my sole care.

And then I somehow fell asleep.

When I woke up, it was almost three o'clock in the afternoon. And Mrs. Pike was with my mother. Mom had had to phone her earlier because she'd needed to take her pills, which were in the kitchen, and she didn't want to wake me. Luckily, Mrs. Pike seemed a lot jollier than she had at the train station at the crack of dawn. (Well, at the time, it had seemed like the crack of dawn, considering it was Saturday.)

"Stacey," said Mom as Mrs. Pike was leaving. "We need to talk."

"Yeah. I guess so."

"You are one of the most mature and reliable thirteen-year-olds I know."

"Thank you."

"But you cannot be everything to everyone."

"I think Dad tried to tell me that this morning," I said, and settled in for a long discussion.

CHAPTER 13

Thursday

Each time I think I have seen everything, something more extraordinary or more humorous or more unbelievable happens. (I guess this is for the best, considering I'm only eleven. I'd hate to think I've already seen all there is to see.) This afternoon I was baby-sitting for Buddy, Suzi, and Marnie. As usual, a bunch of other kids dropped by, including Nicky, Vanessa, and Margo. I expected them to spend the afternoon playing office and ordering free samples through the mail. (Since every last one of them is broke, they can only order free stuff now.) But they didn't open a single magazine or comic book. They had another idea, instead.

By Thursday, the day of Mallory's sitting job at the Barretts' house, my mother was finally better. Sometimes I let her come downstairs for meals. She began to read more, sleep less during the day, and watch less television. On Wednesday when she said she no longer needed someone at the house while I was at school, I said okay, and stopped lining up the neighbors for Mom-sitting. As long as my mother could reach someone by phone she'd be all right. But I still insisted on coming straight home after school and staying there, except when I went to the BSC meeting.

Mal rang the Barretts' bell at three-thirty on Thursday afternoon. Mrs. Barrett herself answered the door, carrying Marnie on her hip.

"Hi," Mal greeted them. "Where are Buddy and Suzi?" Often, they fight over who gets to answer the door.

"They're down in the rec room," replied Mrs. Barrett. "They seem awfully busy, but I'm not sure what they're doing."

"Ooh, mysterious," said Mal. She spoke to Mrs. Barrett for a moment, then took Marnie from her and carried her to the rec room. On the way, she spoke soothingly to Marnie, who sometimes fusses when her mother leaves. "What are your brother and sister doing?" she said. "What are they up to? Are they ordering more things? My brothers and sisters can't do that anymore, you know. They spent all their money. It's gone."

"All gone!" cried Marnie.

Mal smiled. "That's right. All gone."

"Doose?" asked Marnie hopefully.

"You want some juice? Well, in just a minute. First let me see how Buddy and Suzi are doing."

Mallory had heard the front door close by then, and knew Mrs. Barrett had left the house. She was relieved that Marnie had made the transition from Mom to sitter without any tears.

"Kids?" said Mal as she entered the rec room. "Hi, what are you doing?"

"Is Mom gone?" was Buddy's reply.

"Yup."

"Doose?" asked Marnie again.

What a conversation. Mal asked her question again, only this time she tried Suzi. "What are you doing, Suzi?"

Buddy and Suzi were seated on the floor, surrounded by junk.

"This is the stuff we bought," she informed Mal. "Every single thing."

"Our friends are coming over with their stuff," added Buddy.

"Doose?"

"Okay, I'll get you some juice," said Mal,

who still wasn't sure what Buddy and Suzi were *do*ing.

While Mallory was in the kitchen with Marnie, the doorbell rang. Buddy raced to answer it. He let Haley and Matt inside. Presently, Jake Kuhn, Nicky, Vanessa, and Margo arrived. Just as Buddy had said, each came with all the stuff he or she had ordered. The Barretts' rec room looked like a dime store.

The kids were examining their products.

Mal looked at them, too. "So?" she said.

"So we are going to sell this stuff," Buddy told her.

Mal coughed. "Excuse me?"

"We are going to sell everything."

Sell it? Who on earth would buy it? This was the mother of all bad ideas.

"You're going to set up a stand?" asked Mal. "Have a store?"

"Oh, no," said Haley. "Vanessa had a much better idea."

Mallory eyed her sister. "What's your idea?"

"We are going to be salesmen. I mean, salespeople. We are going to travel around the neighborhood with our products. We'll display them in a wagon or something. We'll go to every house. That way, we won't have to wait for people to come to us."

"And you're going to call, 'Get your tiestraightener here!' Things like that?" asked Mal, trying to look serious.

"It's a necktie-*knotter*," said Margo impatiently.

"Whatever," said Mal.

"Better than that," spoke up Nicky. "We're going to put on a show."

"Like those old-time medicine shows," explained Haley, "when people loaded their products onto a cart and went all over the west, giving talks about their amazing medicines and putting on demonstrations."

"Only *we* are going to write songs — " said Nicky.

"*Rap* songs," interrupted Jake.

" — and make up dances — "

"And poems," interrupted Vanessa, who wants to be a poet.

"And maybe even plays," finished up Nicky.

"You're going to sell your stuff by singing rap songs?" Mal was incredulous.

"Yeah. And you know what, you guys?" said Vanessa. "We better get the triplets over here. They have a lot of stuff to sell. But more important, they'd be really good at performing rap songs in our show. I mean, they're *trip*lets. They'd look so cool singing rap. They can dress the same and fix their hair the same.

Now let's see. What could we call them?"

"Don't you think you better find out first if they'll be in the show?" asked Mal. "Maybe they won't want to do it."

"Oh, they will," Vanessa assured her. "They're broke. And they want those yo-yos. The light-up kind, like David Michael's."

However, to be on the safe side, Nicky phoned his brothers, who *did* want to be in the show and said they'd come right over. When they arrived, Buddy greeted them at the door with, "We have to think of a name for you guys. Something better than The Rapping Triplets. That was Suzi's idea."

The triplets joined the other kids in the Barretts' rec room.

"We could call ourselves the Bad Boys," said Adam with a grin, as he settled himself on the floor near Jake.

"Absolutely not," replied Mal.

"How about Rap, Rap, Rap?" suggested Jordan. "Since there are three of us."

"Do we really have to have a name?" asked Byron. "Everybody who's going to sell their stuff is going to perform, right? Not just us triplets."

"Wrong!" cried Haley. "*I'm* not going to perform. I'll write songs or make costumes or something."

"Well, anyway, Adam and Jordan and I are

not the only ones who'll be singing. Other people will, too. I don't think we need a name."

"Okay," said Haley. "Then — " She stopped speaking when she realized Matt was trying to get her attention. He had scooted around so he was sitting in front of her, and now he was signing wildly. "Oh," she said to the others after a moment, "Matt doesn't know what 'rap' means. Now how am I going to explain it to him? You guys keep planning."

Haley turned her full attention to her brother, and they signed back and forth while the other kids continued discussing ideas.

"What about costumes?" asked Jake. "Haley said she'd work on costumes. But what are our costumes?"

"Don't you think you better plan your songs and skits first?" asked Mal. "Then you'll know what costumes you need."

The kids broke into pairs and small groups and divided up the junk they were going to sell. Buddy, always concerned about Matt, tapped Haley on the shoulder. "Is Matt going to be in the show?" he asked. "We can't leave him out."

"Sure he's going to be in it!" answered Haley. "Matt is terrific at pantomine. I'll write some special skits just for him. You can narrate them and Matt can pantomine them."

"Oh, okay." Buddy looked relieved.

Mal let the kids work on their own during the rest of the afternoon. Outside the sky had darkened and a wind had sprung up. The rappers were content to stay inside. While they rhymed words, examined products, and wrote skits, Mal held Marnie in her lap and read to her.

They read *The Runaway Bunny* while the triplets recited, "You got a tie? It's all awry? Then you should try . . ."

They read *Babar's Little Girl* while Haley coached Matt. "Okay, now look really sad. . . . No, sadder. . . . Yeah, almost crying. Now get down on your knees and beg for that crow's feet stuff."

They looked at the pictures in *Good Dog, Carl* while Vanessa said to Margo, "This will be a song with motions. You know, like 'I'm a Little Teapot.' Only the song will be about a girl who falls asleep and dreams she gets a slice 'n' dice for her birthday."

Surprisingly, the kids worked out nearly fifteen songs and skits by the time Mrs. Barrett returned. They decided to take their show on the road on Saturday.

CHAPTER 14

On Friday, my mother ventured out of the house twice. The first time was to bring in the newspaper. She did that while I was in school, so she was dressed — for the first time in a week and a half — when I came home in the afternoon. The second time was to walk through the yards to visit Mrs. Pike. She stayed for nearly an hour. When she came home, which was at the same time I came home from the BSC meeting, she said she felt fine, although she did go to bed awfully early that evening. But on Saturday morning she was up before I was. And later, when I headed for a sitting job with Matt and Haley, Mom said she was going to drive to the grocery store. I knew she would be okay.

I arrived at the Braddocks' house at ten-thirty, and found the kids in a state of great excitement. It was the day of the road show.

I had a very bad feeling about it.

"I hope everybody does a good job," said Haley worriedly.

"I hope I earn my money back," signed Matt.

Mr. and Mrs. Braddock were going to be away until four o'clock that afternoon. They were visiting Mr. Braddock's mother at a nursing home in New Haven, and wanted to spend most of the day with her.

Why did I have a bad feeling about the road show? Not because I thought the kids were badly prepared. Not because I thought they would do a poor job. Nothing like that. Actually, I thought the show was going to be quite good, a lot of fun. It's just that I knew no one would want to buy the junk the kids were selling. I was afraid they'd worked hard and gotten their hopes up for nothing. The day would end and they'd feel tired and discouraged — and maybe embarrassed — and they would still be stuck with the stuff they'd ordered. And no yo-yos. I didn't feel I should say this to Haley and Matt, though.

"When does the road show start?" I asked the kids after their parents had left. (While I spoke, Haley signed to Matt.)

"Well, we're supposed to meet at eleven o'clock at Buddy's," Haley replied. "All of us. I guess the show will start as soon as we're ready."

120

"I'm coming along with you guys today," I pointed out. "I hope you don't mind."

"Oh, no. It'll be fun!" exclaimed Haley. Then, "Wait a sec." She turned to Matt, who was signing to us. "Oh, right!" she cried. "Matt says to remember our costumes. Let's see, we need our Halloween wigs."

"And props," Matt was signing. "The bucket and pail."

Matt and Haley gathered their things together. Fifteen minutes later, Haley said, "Okay, we're ready."

"Where's the stuff you're selling?" I asked.

"Oops."

Matt and Haley loaded their collection of gadgets and bottles and jars into their old red wagon in a messy heap.

"Um, don't you think a display would look, oh, more enticing?" I suggested. (The kids could not afford to be sloppy.)

Haley considered this.

Matt signed, "Get a towel."

The Braddocks lined up their products on an old blue towel spread in the wagon. Then we left their house and headed for Buddy's.

The scene in the Barretts' front yard was pretty interesting: Buddy and his wagon, Jake and Laurel and their wagon, all the Pikes and two wagons (Mal was coming along to help keep an eye on the kids), and now Matt and Haley and their wagon.

Buddy took charge. "Did everybody remember their props and costumes?"

"Yes!"

"Did everybody remember their wagons?" (The answer to this question was obvious, but Buddy liked being in charge.)

"Yes!"

"Did everybody remember their stuff to sell?"

"Yes!"

Then another voice shouted, "Did everybody remember their sisters?"

Buddy turned around. Standing on the front porch steps were Suzi Barrett and Patsy Kuhn. Apparently there had been some disagreement over whether they could take part in the show.

"I bought half of our stuff!" Suzi said indignantly to Buddy. "And I even helped write a song about bust development."

(Vanessa coughed loudly.)

"And *I* bought half of *our* stuff!" shouted Patsy.

"You did not!" Laurel shouted back. "You gave us three quarters."

"You guys are just too little to come with us," said Buddy. "We might go really, really far today."

"How far?"

"To Jessi Ramsey's house."

"That isn't far. Anyway, Claire gets to go."

"Her big sister is coming with her," said Buddy, eyeing Mal.

"How about if I'm everybody's big sister today? I'll be in charge of Claire, Patsy, and Suzi," offered Mal. "If they get tired, I'll take them home."

Buddy kicked at a pebble on the lawn.

"I *did* make up that song," said Suzi.

"Okay, okay, okay," said Buddy. Then he brightened. "All right, everybody. Let's get the show on the road. We will start right here!"

"I'll be the doorbell-ringer!" shouted Margo, sounding hysterical.

"Calm *down*!" whispered Mal loudly.

Margo calmed down enough to ring the Barretts' bell. Presently, Mrs. Barrett opened the door. She was wearing blue jeans and a sweat shirt. An apron was tied around her waist. Marnie, whimpering, was pressing her face into her mother's leg. Mrs. Barrett looked as though the last thing she needed just then was to be interrupted by a bunch of kids selling freckler-remover and bust-developers.

Buddy, holding the handle of his wagon, was standing nearest his mother. He glanced over his shoulder at the other kids, then back at Mrs. Barrett. Finally he picked up the stamp-licker from among the things in the wagon. He held it toward his mother. "Is your tongue dry?" he asked. "Do you write lots of letters? Then this is for you. . . . Just a dollar-fifty," he added when his mother didn't respond.

"Buddy, I — " Mrs. Barrett began to say.

"Doose?" asked Marnie.

"Just a minute, sweetie."

The triplets came to Buddy's rescue. "Don't get sick, don't take a lick. If you gotta write a letter, then this is better. It's Stix, yeah, yeah. You gotta try Stix. . . . Why dontcha try Stix?" The triplets let their voices fade away dramatically.

By the time they had finished, Mrs. Barrett was grinning. "That was great!" she exclaimed. She handed each of the triplets a dime.

Buddy's eyes widened. "Suzi, come here!" he hissed. "Let's do our Mother's Helper play, okay?"

One of the many items Buddy had sent away for was a gadget called Mother's Helper. The ad had said it could pick up dust as well as any vacuum cleaner — and it cost just sixty-nine cents. Mother's Helper was an ordinary dustcloth, as far as I could see.

Suzi, glad to be needed after all, joined her

brother by their wagon. She picked up a broom. She tied an apron around her waist. Then she sagged against Buddy. She nearly slid to the ground.

Buddy adopted an announcer's voice. Speaking into an imaginary microphone, he said, "Does everyday housework make you feel tired and rundown?" He looked at Suzi for a moment, then nudged her.

"Oh!" cried Suzi. "Um, goodness, I am so tired. How will I finish my everyday housework *and* go to the office?"

"You could try Mother's Helper," said Buddy brightly. "It takes the work out of housework." Buddy glanced at his mother to see if she appreciated the creativity of that line. "Just slip Mother's Helper onto your hand — " (Suzi did so) " — and cleaning becomes a snap." Buddy waited a moment, then had to nudge his sister again.

"Oh! Um — goodness, I feel so much better. With Mother's Helper I can finish my housework in half the time, and it doesn't even feel like work!"

Buddy and Suzi took bows, indicating that their performance was over.

Their mother clapped her hands. "Wonderful!" she exclaimed. She handed dimes to Buddy and Suzi.

Buddy held the Mother's Helper toward Mrs. Barrett. "Just sixty-nine cents," he reminded her hopefully.

"Well," she replied.

The triplets handed her Buddy's stamp-licker. "Just a dollar-fifty," said Byron. "Cheap at twice the price."

"Well. . . . I guess not," Mrs. Barrett admitted. "But I loved the show."

"You did?" said Buddy. "Honest?"

Mrs. Barrett nodded. "It really is wonderful."

"Let's go to my house!" said Vanessa, a gleam in her eye.

So the road show organized itself into a caravan of red wagons. The kids walked along the sidewalk to the Pikes' yard and up their driveway. Margo rang the bell.

"I hope someone's home," Mal whispered to me. "Most of us Pikes are out here with the show."

But a moment later, both of her parents had opened the door. (I suspected they'd been watching us from a window.)

"Heavenly days!" exclaimed Mal's father, as if he knew nothing whatsoever about the road show.

Mal put her head in her hands. "I can't believe he just said that," she muttered, and I replied, "*My* father says 'I swan.' "

"What have we here?" asked Mrs. Pike.

Immediately, the triplets were in action. Byron held up a small glass jar and he and his brothers chanted, "Get, get, get Wrinkle-Away. Yo, yo, get Wrinkle-Away."

I stifled a giggle.

When the rap song ended, Mr. Pike was grinning. He gave each of the triplets a quarter. Inspired, Matt and Nicky performed a commercial for Lawn Buddy, a product hailed as "the answer to all your gardening problems."

Mrs. Pike gave each of *them* a quarter.

But nobody actually wanted to buy the Wrinkle-Away or the Lawn Buddy.

All morning long, this happened. We trooped from one house to the next. The kids gave memorable performances, for which they earned money. But they could not unload any of the products.

We stopped at Mary Anne and Dawn's house. Dawn's mom rewarded the kids for their inaccurate but humorous play about "bust development." As we were leaving, Dawn decided to join our caravan.

We went to Bradford Court where, before we could even approach the Kishis' house, we attracted an audience right on the sidewalk. We were surrounded by kids — including the Perkins girls, the Hobart boys, Jamie Newton, and several other clients of the BSC.

Of course, they didn't want to buy anything — until Jake brought out his vial of moondust. Before he could even perform his elaborately choreographed Moondust Walk, James Hobart cried, "I'll buy that! I'll pay three dollars for it!"

"Sold!" said Jake.

Buddy held up his moondust. Myriah Perkins bought it.

"I want moondust!" exclaimed Jamie Newton.

Margo sold him hers.

"I want moondust, too!" cried a kid I didn't even know.

We all looked at Suzi.

"Where's your moondust?" Buddy asked his sister.

"Hiding," she replied. "It isn't for sale. I am one of twenty special people. I am *keeping* my moondust."

And that was the end of that.

Not long after lunch, the youngest children — Claire, Suzi, and Patsy — grew whiny, so Mallory took them home. The older kids continued their traveling road show. They kept going until I told Matt and Haley it was time for them to go home, too. Their parents would be back soon. So the show came to an end. The kids were stuck with most of their products but they had earned enough money for plenty of yo-yos. They decided to take the show to a different neighborhood the next weekend.

CHAPTER 15

"Claud, what's that?" I asked. I pointed to my friend's dressing table.

"That? It's just lipstick," she replied.

"No, what's next to it? That little pink tube?"

Claudia blushed. "Well, it's this stuff to get rid of crow's feet. I bought it from Haley Braddock."

"You don't have crow's feet!"

"Well, actually, I think I might. Look right here."

I peered at Claud's face. It was as smooth as glass. "Not a wrinkle in sight. Claud, you're only thirteen. . . . Hey, what's *that*?"

"Oh, it's Wrinkle-Away."

"Claudia! I suppose you bought it from the Pikes?"

"Yeah. The traveling road show came through the neighborhood again yesterday and I couldn't resist. Anyway, I'd been looking in the mirror the other day and I noticed that when I smile I *do* get wrinkles around my eyes. Real wrinkles. Or crow's feet. I wasn't sure which. See? Watch this."

Claudia smiled (not very convincingly) and I could see what she meant. "Those are called laugh lines," I informed her. "Even babies get them. Your skin has to go *some*where when you smile. It's, like, a law of physics."

"I didn't know you could apply physics to cosmetology."

"Don't change the subject, Claud."

"Well, I don't want to look old, so when that road show came by again — right to our door this time — and I heard that song about crow's feet and that play about Wrinkle-Away, I decided not to resist anymore. I just couldn't. I felt I was putting my face in danger."

It was a Friday afternoon. The BSC meeting wouldn't start for about half an hour, and Claud and I had no sitting jobs or other plans. So we were just hanging out in her room.

"It's nice to have you here," Claud said several moments later.

"What?"

"Well, when your mom was sick you were so busy we only saw each other in school and at meetings. You didn't have time to relax. You couldn't come over just to visit."

"Yeah. Those weeks were kind of rough."

"But they're over now."

"Yup."

My mother had fully recovered. The surest sign of this was that our house was back to normal. Not just clean, but orderly. I may never understand Mom's knack for keeping things running smoothly. Maybe it's a talent that develops with age. Or with parenthood. At any rate, I was a kid again, concentrating on school and baby-sitting. And Mom was my mom again, looking for a job, temping, and holding our little family together. Mrs. Pike still dropped by for visits, but the Mom-sitting chart (which I had located behind my desk where it had fallen) had been thrown away. My mother wasn't even taking medicine anymore.

By 5:20, the other members of the BSC had arrived for the meeting. Kristy, the last to show up, since she's at the mercy of Charlie's schedule, was grinning at me. She continued to grin at me as she settled into the director's chair.

"What's so funny?" I asked her.

"Nothing. . . . This meeting of the Baby-sitters Club will now come to order."

"Kristy! You keep smiling at me," I exclaimed. Honestly, sometimes she can be so immature. Or at least frustrating.

Kristy stuck a pencil over her ear. "I just

found out Sam's plans for Saturday night," she said. (Sometimes Kristy does this annoying thing where she only tells, like, half a story so her listeners are forced to ask her questions.)

Mary Anne played right into her hand. "Saturday night?"

"Sam has a date," said Kristy.

"With?" prompted Jessi.

Kristy looked at me.

Suddenly everyone was punching my arms and crying, "Ooh, Stacey!"

Now I was grinning. "He finally called," I admitted. "I didn't want to say anything because I was afraid it would jinx our da — our night. I mean, when Mom was sick, and I couldn't walk home with Sam that time, and we barely talked on the phone, I thought I'd blown it. But tomorrow night we're going to a movie."

"Cool," said Dawn.

The phone began to ring and we arranged a few sitting jobs. After Mal had finished talking to Mrs. Barrett she said, "Um, Claud, I couldn't help but notice. Isn't that Jordan's Wrinkle-Away? That jar on your dresser next to the — the crow's feet remover?"

My friends and I began to laugh.

"Okay, okay," said Claud. "So the kids are good salespeople."

"How much of their stuff have they gotten rid of?" asked Kristy.

"Just a little," said Mal. "But they've earned back most of their money. They're good performers, too."

"Have they bought their yo-yos?" asked Dawn.

Mal nodded. "Yup. And not just my brothers and sisters. So did Matt, Haley, Buddy, Jake, and a few others. They bought the light-up kind, like David Michael's."

"Yesterday," spoke up Jessi, "I was sitting at the Kuhns' and Jake said something about a neighborhood yo-yo tournament."

"The next big project," commented Mary Anne.

"Children," said Kristy, "are never boring."

"Another Deep Thought from Kristin Amanda Thomas," I said.

When the meeting ended a few minutes later, my friends left Claud's room. Claudia stood at the front door of her house and waved as the rest of us headed for our bicycles (except for Kristy, who headed for Charlie's car). Then Jessi rode off in one direction, and Mary Anne, Dawn, Mal, and I rode off in another. By the time I reached my driveway, it was almost dark.

Mom was waiting for me at our door.

"Hi!" I called to her. "See you inside!"

I locked my bicycle in the garage and entered our house through the side door.

"Hi, honey," said Mom.

"Hi. Yum. Dinner smells good. Hey, the dining room table is set. How come?" (We use the dining room only for special or fancy occasions.)

"You'll see."

Dinner that night was salad, vegetable stew, and cornbread. Mom and I ate at opposite sides of the table, two lighted candles between us.

"So? Are we celebrating something?" I asked.

"Maybe."

"You got a job?" I exclaimed. "Is that it? You got a job?"

"Maybe."

"Mo-*om*! Tell me. You're acting like Kristy."

Mom smiled. "I mean that maybe I got a job. Remember when I was interviewing for the buyer's job at Bellair's Department Store?"

"Yeah."

"And another interview had been scheduled, but I missed it because I was sick?"

"Yeah? . . . Hey, wait Mom. You didn't faint during the *Bellair's* interview, did you? That's not where you were when you collapsed, is it? I mean, because I don't think that would be a very good recommendation for you as a future employee. Fainting on your boss's floor."

"No," said Mom, laughing. "I missed the Bellair's interview entirely. And later, when I called the woman to tell her what had happened and that I'd be laid up for awhile, I really didn't expect to hear from her again. But she called while you were at Claudia's, and she was delighted to hear I'm all well. She set up the interview for Monday, and she even asked me how soon I'd be able to start working."

"Oh, Mom, that is so fantastic!" I cried. "Hey, find out about the employee discount. I'm sure you get one, even if you aren't a salesperson." I raised my glass to Mom. "Congratulations," I said seriously.

"Thank you," she replied.

"When are you going to tell Dad?"

"As soon as it's official. . . . Speaking of your father, have *you* talked to him recently, Stace?"

"Me? Well, no."

"Not since you saw him in New York?"

"No."

"A lot of time has passed, honey. Maybe you should call him."

"I guess. I do have something to tell him."

"What's that?"

"What I learned when you were sick. I

didn't figure it out at first. But later I realized something about my decision not to make a decision. Remember that? Remember when I thought *not* choosing between you and Dad would be easier than making a choice? So I decided to please both of you that weekend. Only you know what? That turned out to be even more complicated. I was in a huge rush. I ruined Dad's evening. I scheduled your Mom-sitters sloppily and they all showed up at once. Then I sent them home and I fell asleep and you had to ask Mrs. Pike to come back. I didn't even pack well. My outfit got smushed and Dad and I arrived late to the dinner because I had to iron everything."

"You know, Stacey, Dad and I appreciate that you try to do what's best," said Mom, "but don't always try to please *us*. Remember to please yourself. I don't mean you should act selfishly, but don't forget about Stacey McGill. She's an important person, too."

"I know. It's just that after a divorce, the rules change. I don't always know what to do. The game is different now."

"It's different for your father and me, as well," said Mom.

I would remember that. When I wrote the Divorce Handbook I would title one of the chapters "Different Rules," or something like that.

"Well, maybe I will call Dad tonight," I said finally.

"Good. I know he'll like that."

I was going to phone my father right away, but as I was dialing, I got an idea. I stopped dialing. I hung up the phone. I opened my calendar and located my next free weekend. I hoped it was free for Dad, too.

Then I picked up the phone again, only I called Claudia. "Hi," I said. "Can you help me with something? Could you design a certificate? . . . No, bigger than that. One you could frame and hang on your wall. I want to make an award for my father. The Fantastic Father Award."

I had decided to plan an award ceremony all my own for Dad. I would fix him a dinner and make a speech about him and give him the first annual Fantastic Father certificate.

I would be sure to tell him how much I love him.

I dialed a number on the phone. "Hi, Dad?" I said. "It's me, Stacey."

About the Author

ANN M. MARTIN did *a lot* of baby-sitting when she was growing up in Princeton, New Jersey. She is a former editor of books for children, and was graduated from Smith College.

Ms. Martin lives in New York City with her cats, Mouse and Rosie. She likes ice cream and *I Love Lucy*; and she hates to cook.

Ann Martin's Apple Paperbacks include *Yours Turly, Shirley*; *Ten Kids, No Pets*; *With You and Without You*; *Bummer Summer*; and all the other books in the Baby-sitters Club series.

Look for #59

MALLORY HATES BOYS (AND GYM)

The next thing I knew Robbie was leaping in front of me, hurling himself at the ball. His arm jabbed me in the side. His foot came down hard on mine. Suddenly I lost my balance and was flying over backwards. I landed with a thud on the gym floor.

And was everyone all concerned about me? Oh, no! They were cheering because we had finally made a point!

"Pike, are you okay?" asked Ms. Walden, who was moving from game to game.

I didn't know which was worse, the pain in my foot, or the embarrassment. Hot tears tingled just below my eyes, but I didn't want anyone to see them. "I'm all right," I mumbled, climbing to my feet.

"Get in there after that ball," she told me. "You're wimping out on your team."

Thanks for making that so clear, I thought

140

bitterly. Just in case anyone here wasn't aware of that.

Once my team had the ball it wasn't so bad. At least every serve wasn't directed at me. And I discovered that if I hopped up and down with my arms in the air, I could pretend to be a functioning member of the team.

I didn't fool Ms. Walden, though. "Pike! Don't just flap your arms!" she'd yell. "This is your ball, Pike! Get it!"

So, thanks to Ms. Walden's big mouth, all eyes were on me every time the ball flew past me.

The game seemed endless. I couldn't help but wonder what terrible thing I'd done to deserve this torture.

The girls on my team weren't too bad. They weren't that into it. But the boys were total animals! You'd think they were engaged in a war, the way they yelled, leaped, pounded the ball, and spiked it over the net. Didn't they realize it was just a game?

After what seemed like a thousand years, the game ended. As I slunk off the court, I realized Jessi had been right. Gym hadn't been as bad as I thought.

It had been much worse.

**Read all the latest books
in the Baby-sitters Club series
by Ann M. Martin**

142

#52 *Mary Anne + 2 Many Babies*
Who ever thought taking care of a bunch of babies could be so much trouble?

#53 *Kristy for President*
Can Kristy run the BSC and the whole eighth grade?

#54 *Mallory and the Dream Horse*
Mallory is taking professional riding lessons. It's a dream come true!

#55 *Jessi's Gold Medal*
Jessi's going for the gold in a synchronized swimming competition!

#56 *Keep Out, Claudia!*
Who wouldn't want Claudia for a baby-sitter?

#57 *Dawn Saves the Planet*
Dawn's trying to do a good thing — but she's driving everyone crazy!

#58 *Stacey's Choice*
Stacey's parents are both depending on her. But how can she choose between them . . . again?

#59 *Mallory Hates Boys (and Gym)*
Boys and gym. What a disgusting combination!

Super Specials:
4 *Baby-sitters' Island Adventure*
Two of the Baby-sitters are shipwrecked!

5 *California Girls!*
A winning lottery ticket sends the Baby-sitters to *California*!

6 *New York, New York!*
Bloomingdales, the Hard Rock Cafe — the BSC is going to see it all!

 # 7 *Snowbound*
Stoneybrook gets hit by a major blizzard. Will the Baby-sitters be okay?

 # 8 *The Baby-sitters at Shadow Lake*
Campfires, cute guys, *and* a mystery — the Baby-sitters are in for a week of summer fun!

Mysteries:
 # 3 *Mallory and the Ghost Cat*
Mallory finds a spooky white cat. Could it be a ghost?

 # 4 *Kristy and the Missing Child*
Kristy organizes a search party to help the police find a missing child.

 # 5 *Mary Anne and the Secret in the Attic*
Mary Anne discovers a secret about her past and now she's afraid of the future!

 # 6 *The Mystery at Claudia's House*
Claudia's room has been ransacked! Can the Baby-sitters track down whodunnit?

Special Edition (Readers' Request):
Logan's Story
Being a boy baby-sitter isn't easy!

THE BABY-SITTERS CLUB®

by Ann M. Martin

The Baby-sitters Club titles continued...

Available wherever you buy books...or use this order form.

Scholastic Inc., P.O. Box 7502, 2931 E. McCarty Street, Jefferson City, MO 65102

Please send me the books I have checked above. I am enclosing $ _____
(please add $2.00 to cover shipping and handling). Send check or money order - no cash or C.O.D.s please.

Name _____

Address _____

City_____ State/Zip _____

Please allow four to six weeks for delivery. Offer good in the U.S. only. Sorry, mail orders are not available to residents of Canada. Prices subject to change.

BSC1291

Enter **THE BABY-SITTERS CLUB** ®

WIN A LOCKET CHARM BRACELET!

Super Special Trivia Giveaway

10 WINNERS

Take the Baby-sitters Club trivia challenge! Answer all the questions correctly and you have the chance to win a beautiful locket charm bracelet. Just fill in this entry page with the correct answers and return by November 30, 1992.

15 SECOND PRIZE WINNERS get Baby-sitters Club portable cassette players!
25 THIRD PRIZE WINNERS get Baby-sitters Club carry cassette players!

Fill in the blanks with the correct baby-sitter's name!

1. She has always lived on Bradford Court. _____
2. She is originally from New York City. _____
3. Baseball is her favorite sport. _____
4. She helped Jackie Rodowsky build a volcano for a science project. _____
5. She burns easily at the beach. _____
6. She has two pierced holes in each ear. _____
7. She would like to be an author. _____

Rules: Entries must be postmarked by November 30, 1992. Winners will be picked at random and notified by mail. No purchase necessary. Void where prohibited. Valid only in the U. S. and Canada. Taxes on prizes are the responsibility of the winners and their immediate families. Employees of Scholastic Inc.; its agencies, affiliates, subsidiaries; and their immediate families are not eligible. For a complete list of winners, send a self-addressed stamped envelope to: The Baby-sitters Club Super Special Trivia Giveaway, Winners List, at the address provided below.

Fill in this entry page and the coupon below or write the information on a 3" x 5" piece of paper and mail to: THE BABY-SITTERS CLUB SUPER SPECIAL TRIVIA GIVEAWAY, P.O. Box 7500, Jefferson City, MO 65102. Canadian residents send entries to: Iris Ferguson, Scholastic Inc., 123 Newkirk Road, Richmond Hill, Ontario, Canada L4C365.

Name_____ Age_____

Street_____

City_____ State_____ Zip_____

Where did you buy this *Baby-sitters Club* book?

❑ Bookstore   ❑ Drugstore   ❑ Supermarket   ❑ Library
❑ Book Club   ❑ Book Fair   ❑ Other_____(specify)

BSC192

Don't miss out!

Join the
BABY-SITTERS
Fan Club!

Pssst... Know what? You can find out **everything** there is to know about *The Baby-sitters Club*. Join the BABY-SITTERS FAN CLUB! Get the hot news on the series, the inside scoop on all the Baby-sitters, and lots of baby-sitting fun...just for $4.95!

With your **two-year** membership, you get:

☆ An official membership card!
☆ A colorful banner!
☆ The exclusive Baby-sitters Fan Club quarterly newsletter with baby-sitting tips, activities and more!

Just fill in the coupon below and mail with payment to:
THE BABY-SITTERS FAN CLUB,
Scholastic Inc., P.O. Box 7500, 2931 E. McCarty Street, Jefferson City, MO 65012.

The Baby-sitters Fan Club

❑ **YES!** Enroll me in The Baby-sitters Fan Club! I've enclosed my check or money order (no cash please) for $4.95 made payable to Scholastic Inc.

Name _____ Age _____

Street _____

City _____ State/Zip _____

Where did you buy this *Baby-sitters Club* book?

❑ Bookstore   ❑ Drugstore   ❑ Supermarket   ❑ Book Club
❑ Book Fair   ❑ Other_____(specify)
Not available outside of U.S. and Canada.